Archangels And Demons

Romance

Archangels And Demons

Abdenal Carvalho

Title: Archangels and Demons

Category: Horror

Author's cover designer

Author Review

Author's Translation

Format: "6 x9" / 3st Edition / 112 pages

Published Date: 11/2020

This is a work of fiction. Your goal is to amuse people. Names, people, places and events described are products of the author's imagination. Any similarity to real names, dates and events is purely coincidental.

This work follows the rules of the New Spelling of the Portuguese Language. Everything will be reserved.

SUMMARY

Prologue

My name was João Batista, I was born in an unbelieving family about the evil that surrounded me and one day I discovered that I was the son of the evil one, something that I only knew after much being tormented by those dark beings. That morning, like many others, they came to meet me while I was terrified.

I remained wrapped in an old hammock, made of coarse cloth, with a bad smell due to several months without being washed, it was possible to hear their footsteps going towards the place where I was shaking with fear of the terrifying touch of those repulsive beings. With the mentality of a child just eight years old, he understood nothing.

I was unable to understand that they were disincarnated spirits, the demons, coming directly from the darkness to torment me, with me, at a short distance, my brother was three years older than me, but he did not notice anything. He slept soundly while the terror of that damned chase kept me from sleeping all night.

Worst of all, at dawn neither he nor any member of my family gave credence to my reports, for them they were nothing more than the fanciful stories of a fearful boy who was terrified of his own shadow. That martyrdom under the power of darkness that haunted me throughout my childhood.

Adolescence and youth was terrible, they touched me all over my body, their icy hands slid over me from head to toe. They tickled my ribs, under my feet, they blew on my ears. They seemed to have fun listening to my calls for help in a sound that only they could hear, I became a kind of amusement for those damn dark beings who seemed to have come out of the depths of the abyss to torment me.

I saw them clearly, there were five demonic beings who visited me every night. They made my life a living hell with their irritating games, they seemed to want to do me no harm, just to have fun with my agony. They laughed all the time, they had fun when they saw me screaming, knowing that it would do no good, because the one who was in tears was my innocent soul and the sound of my voice was silenced.

No one would listen, they would not help, no help would get me out of that sinister and terrifying spectacle, it lasted for a long time, for many years I lived with the sons of the evil one surrounding me everywhere, every time I tried to sleep.

First Chapter: Torments

My family has always been rejected by the residents of the small town where we lived, since I was born there was not a single visit from neighbors, relatives or anyone else, not even my uncles frequented our house due to rumors that my father was an extreme sorcerer.

And that it was enough to determine the death of someone and individual turned into ham, but you can be sure that this was a profound truth, Dad struggled with that kind of thing, occult sciences, good witchcraft, he never left a single client dissatisfied with the jobs ordered.

I think that was why the demons roamed freely in the rooms of our house, tormented me all the time as if I were a chosen one. I remember the many times I tried to convince my parents and brothers of the constant persecution by the evil spirits.

But in vain, they even made fun of me, for them it was all pure fear and cowardice of a kid who still urinated in the hammock. For this reason, I remained at the mercy of evil beings. I punished like a convict without finding any way to get rid of that terrible situation. Because whenever the day ended and a new night started, the torment was certain. They came to tease me, hurt my soul, scream in my ears, tickle my palms, make me crazy! On one of the many occasions of anguish, when the dawn ended the night and the first signs of a new day appeared.

I was already too tired from the several hours of being tortured, I got up. I jumped from the net in a jump, not understanding where I got so much courage from, running out of there and went to the house next door where my parents and two older sisters were, screaming for help. In the face of my despair, they could then see that my supposed hints about an alleged persecution by demons were true.

— My God, child, but what's going on?

— What is this business about punching the door of the house in the middle of the night boy, did you happen to go crazy?

— Calm down, José, don't you see that the boy is terrified?

— Again this stupid story of demons? This kid is deserving is a good spanking!

— Do not even dare to beat my son, if he is so scared it is because something must have happened! Come, my child, lie here with Dad and Mom ...

— It was just what I needed ...

— Stop murmuring, man, what a thing!

That remainder at dawn would have been quiet if the dark beings were not so bold as to go looking for me. There, even with my parents, lying between the two of them and wrapped their feet from head to toe, I was not even safe from the evil ones, because soon after everything returned to silence and the couple slept peacefully. I returned to feeling that usual chill that indicated the presence of beings from the other world. There, I thought, they are here to torment me!

I didn't even have time to scream, my tongue got stuck in my mouth and my skeletal body could no longer move, only my ears could hear the crawling of his steps. They came towards the bed and the eyes of my soul were able to visualize each of them in their most chilling forms.

They stood in front of the bed, looking at me wryly, as if mocking the dread that would certainly be stamped on my face, paired, side by side, before our feet. The first appeared to have been a soldier who fought in the war, as he wore a green army uniform, but all torn and dirty.

Everything indicated that he had been killed on the battlefield and became a lost soul, he kept laughing, it was the bastard who tickled my feet and ribs. Another was big, tall, huge. His trick was to put his long hands inside my shorts and squeeze my testicles until they popped completely.

Yes, the unfortunate man did that to me every night and was amused by my bitter pain, however it was just an illusion, it seems that it was only my soul that suffered that torture, because upon awakening nothing had happened, my grains were intact. The woman dressed in red looked like a prostitute.

I always smoked a cigarette that apparently never went out or came to an end, she kept looking at me and in the space of each drink she smiled sadly, giving the impression of feeling satisfaction with my suffering. Their room carried a small, sharp ax in his right hand, several times he cut my neck high. The fifth was black. Hundreds of times I saw my head rolling on the floor of the house, it was an amazing thing to have my head ripped from the body

And by the eyes of the soul to see it being thrown on the floor, the fifth was the ugliest and most perverse, this would have been at some point in its existence a very evil arsonist, because it burned me alive several times in the burning flames.

While it was dawn they began to practice their evils with me without my parents noticing any sudden movement of my body stretched out on the bed, among them, apparently calm, giving the impression that I would be in deep sleep.

At that time there were several flashes to which I was transported inexplicably. In one of them I found myself tied to a wooden post, surrounded by a fire whose fire was so high that it covered the whole view around, but it was possible to see that there would be a huge number of people watching everything.

They shouted, blasphemed, seemed to like it to see me burning. The flames licked my inert body, melting little by little, even though it was something that occurred only during a spiritual and not a physical vision, the pain felt to be real, the burning of the burns in my flesh was true, leading to exhaustion in the face of such martyrdom.

Then I was transported to another scenario where I found myself tied by the ankles to a rope, standing upside down. The dark spirit of greater stature. With his long hands, he gripped my scrotums tightly and squeezed them so hard that they burst, I could feel them breaking, the pain was once again unbearable. But it was not possible to faint or die, as our souls do not enter these two states reserved only for the human body, at one point I found myself lying in a hammock.

That was armed in the backyard of the house where I lived, the five demons rocked me with a strong impulse, from side to side, while I could feel my back hitting something that looked like a pile of clay. When I stood up a little I realized that it was a grave and I was overcome with terror.

They laughed and talked among themselves, the sound of their voices was horrible, made by a kind of high-pitched squeak. Terrible, disgusting, suddenly in seconds I was back in bed with my parents. The gloomy ones stood again in front of the bed in the bedroom.

Now half lit by the light of the sun's rays outside, because it was already dawn, little by little their images began to fade as if they were mists, they were dissipated before my frightened gaze and still frozen due to the paralysis that occurred in my body due to the presence of the five amazing beings.

As soon as the paralyzing effect had passed and it was possible to move and open my mouth, I screamed so loudly that Dad was startled. Turning in my direction, he beat me in various parts of my skinny body despite my mother's pleas in my favor, he was beside himself and totally mad with rage. As the new day had already dawned, he went to work and she advised me to stop being afraid.

— My son, stop this nonsense, you only saw what gave your father a screaming wake. I know something is bothering you, but you need to control yourself. Sometimes I think you were born with a head problem

— It's Mom, he's crazy! — My older sister shouted

— I'm not crazy!

— That's what it looks like, you troubled man!

— Stop this fight now, you three, or I'll lose my temper!

— Mom, you don't believe me, but it is true they exist and come every night to get me, they are ugly, they hurt me all night

— Ho, my boy, I'm very worried about you

— You have to put this crazy person in a madhouse!

— Mom, look at her!

— I already ordered to stop the provocations!

— The lady always defending the freshness of this kid just because he is the youngest! — Complained Joaquim, my brother three years older than me

— Yeah, and if I hear one of you complaining about it again, I'll slap you!

The discussion comes to an end and I am dissatisfied with the defense that I usually received from Mom, the others go out the door without saying anything more about the subject, as for me, I was preparing to face another night.

When those damn dark spirits would come to torment me again, despite spending nearly an hour on my knees, praying to the God of heaven and recommending my life to him.

Asking for his protection, requiring him to send an angel who could stop the action of the five dark beings against me, it was useless.They always came and tormented me.

Took me in spirit to different places and did what they liked with me, that is, with my poor soul. Several times I was drowned, strangled, torn, I had both eyes hollowed out, buried alive and under the ground I found myself dying slowly, without air to breathe.

In these cases, I would prefer everything to be real, in fact to die for real, putting an end to that cursed and suffering existence. I hated life, hated everything it had in store for me, hated it from my birth until the day I died, because I believed things would never change, they would always be that way.

At ten years of age I was still persecuted by them, however, things got even worse, because I started to see them during the day, awake, at that time of events it was no longer necessary for the night to arrive even if I was in the hammock, they they passed right in front of me, paraded side by side and I could see them naturally.

I saw them passing by around me, walking through the corridors, in the yard, in the courtyard of the house where we lived, standing leaning against the trees, sitting in a chair right next to us, when we were at the lunch or dinner table. Living with those aberrations became routine, I was no longer scared by their constant appearances.

They only manifested, surrounded me, spent twenty-four hours by my side, no longer harassed me, stopped the martyrdoms, the transitions from one macabre scenario to another, the boring tickling and all other types of disturbance came to an end. However, I started to feel as if they were influencing me, it was as if they were inducing me to do evil. To start, I started to collect cigarette leftovers in the streets.

Put everything in a bag and went to smoke them hidden at the bottom of the property, which was a huge place, hidden among the many trees. At the age of twelve, I was not only smoking but I also tasted and became addicted to alcoholic beverages.

And it wasn't beers or anything like that, my business was really cachaça, I got the drink from Pedro, a colleague I met during my wanderings, it was he who gave me the first dose, I thought it was horrible, but the woman in red came to me in a demonic vision, touched me and said that from that moment I would like alcohol.

They came and went before my eyes, walked side by side with me, we became like friends, I no longer feared their macabre appearances, I got used to the presence of those five beings from hell, I liked to talk to them. I was always a strange boy, weird compared to other children, he liked to be isolated, spoke little and detested chatty people.

At home, no one went to school because Dad understood that there was no need for studies to live, claimed he was illiterate and got a great job at a federal company as a supplier of used fuel in government vehicles. In that way we were all flocks of donkeys, without any education, raised like irrational animals.

Without any perspective on a better future than that miserable present in which we lived. Outside, other people despised us for living in such a way, similar to wild animals. That way I didn't have any friends, nor did I receive invitations to go to someone's house, at a simple birthday party or to throw a ball with the kids, in fact, my father was so late that he said football was an act of violence where the players beat.

Found everything without a future, he hated the sport and if we dared to practice it it was for sure beating. So, we were never sportsmen, our fun was to invent certain pranks on the spot or climb trees to harvest ripe fruit to eat. This generated in me a personality indifferent to the importance of other people and did not give them any value, being attracted to living with the beings of darkness.

Day after day I let myself get involved, I followed his advice, finally dominated my mind, directed my steps towards their paths, induced me to do exactly what they would like to practice if they had a physical body like I had. Smoking, drinking alcohol, and after a while I started wanting sex.

An immense fire started to exist in my testicles, an uncontrollable heat kept my penis erect all the time, making me want to stick it in some hole that was hot and humid like a woman's vagina, which would not take long to happen. presence of so many sluts in a whorehouse located nearby.

— Mom, I need to tell you something very serious!

— What was Maria?

— It's about João's crazy, mom

— Don't treat your brother like that, girl!

— Do what if he is really crazy? And you don’t even know what he’s been up to on the sly

— It is what it is? Come on, girl, speak up!

— That crazy guy is smoking and drinking cachaça!

— How is it? But what a most absurd thing this is, my daughter.

Your brother is only twelve, he doesn't even know what these things are!

— The lady who thinks, Dona Ana, your dear little boy is addicted. I just caught him hiding there at the end of the land smoking and drinking cachaça, come on I'll show you ...

— Well, come on, I want to see this with my own eyes!

Damn it, that time I took it easy and got caught with my mouth in the jar, Mom proved the accusations made by my sister to be true and I took a tremendous beating from her to the point of rolling my eyes after a long sequence of lashes all over the body with branches of a tree, that really hurt.

After the repeated beatings she still made me bathe with water and salt, I was treated like sun meat so that the wounds would not ignite, it was a week of dressing. During this period the five mischievous beings kept me company by the side of my hammock.

We talked about several things, one of them was about who they were and why they chose me to be tormented, that's when I started to understand a little about what happened after death. The one who dressed as a soldier told me that they were not demons, but lost spirits, everyone had lived on earth as people and had no right to salvation.

He made a surprising revelation to me, said he was called José like my father, he had served in the army at the time of the war between Brazil and Paraguay, there was no luck there and he was killed in combat in an explosion.

Caused by a bomb, that's why it appeared to me dressed like that, in combatant's clothes, all torn. But his revelation went further.

— My name is José because I have the same name as my father, that is, our father

— What do you mean, our father?

— Have you ever seen a picture on the wall of the room with the image of a soldier, wearing a green uniform and a hat over his head?

— Yes daddy said he was our older brother who ... My goodness, it's you!

— Yes, I was the first child of our parents, they called me to war and I did not survive

— Cruz credo, what a hairy story! And why the hell was it not accepted up there?

— I was a bad son, disobedient to our parents, I became addicted to drugs, alcohol and fell into prostitution. I was only recruited to serve my homeland due to a lack of contingent, they took anyone and ordered war.

— So you didn't even have time to ask dad or mother for forgiveness?

— No, it was all too fast. As the splinters of the explosion tore through my belly and I saw my viscera exposed outside, I felt my blood emptying my veins and death approaching to take me to the other side. It was at that time that I realized that I should have said goodbye to our parents and got along with them, but it was too late.

— And what is it like to die, my brother?

Tell me how it was to move from side to side!

— Well, in my case I was feeling life slowly disappearing from my body, my eyes started to lose their brightness, everything started to get dark, things around me disappeared and in her place there was only tremendous darkness. Suddenly it clarified and I realized I was there, still lying on the ground, in the same place where the explosion occurred where there were many combatants all over the place, all wounded, broken, torn, some without arms and others without legs, but alive as well as I was too, our condition was terrible, but no one seemed to be in pain or dead.

— My goodness, and you didn't feel any pain either?

— No, I noticed my belly was torn in half, my intestines were partly inside and the other spread out on the floor, but it didn't seem to make any difference

— And what happened next?

— Then I got up and went in an unknown direction, along a path that led me towards a shadow that remained standing at a certain distance, as if waiting for me.

— Was it death?

— It was an evil being that was sent to lead me to hell, came from darkness to take me into the captivity of lost souls

— This happens to all those who are not worthy of light or salvation due to their many sins — adds the giant with huge hands

— Did you all go through this?

— Yes, all the people who were or will be killed will go through this, after awakening from physical death they will be led by dark beings to the darkness or by heavenly angels to the heavens

— Wait, are you telling me that we get out of the body and someone is already there waiting to take us to heaven or to hell?

— That's right, my little brother, start preparing for one day to come meet us

— As well? I don't want to go into the dark or live with you, are you crazy?

— The father of darkness chose you and put the five of us by your side to make you follow our steps, commit all kinds of sin and be rejected by God, so that you can be taken into the darkness where he eagerly awaits you

— Oh my God! You can't do this to me, brother!

— We are sorry, boy, we are obliged to carry out our orders, the father of darkness dominates us, we have no will of our own — said the woman

— But why is he so interested in me?

— He just wants you to come home — warned the giant — If you don't remember you were one of us before you were born in this house and in this family

— Hey, wait a minute, do you mean I was once a lost soul just like you? That I have lived in hell and served the Devil?

— In fact you were one of the most beloved children for him

— Son? But what madness is this now?

— My brother let me explain something to you: There are the children of God and the children of Satan, they are souls created by the Most High, but who commit more sins on earth than others, they commit so many iniquities that in the darkness he is recognized and admired by the father of demons, so he looks forward to their deaths and when they pass to the other side he takes them to his kingdom, in darkness, there he makes them his children, heirs, princes of darkness. This happened to you, spent several centuries beside him, commanding his demons, managing evil in the lives of human beings, but one day the God of the entire Universe determined his return to this world, taking on a new physical form, being born in this family .

— Mercy! So your mission is to guarantee my return to hell?

— Exactly! And for that it is necessary that you commit the same sins and crimes committed in the previous life so that the Creator of souls will refuse you in Paradise

— But you bastards are you! They came in charge of making me sin!

They started to laugh, the sound of their laughter was amazing and made me shiver, everything about them was dark and terrifying, it gave the impression that the prince of darkness himself lived inside each one of them. Shortly after that long conversation, they disappeared and spent days without me being able to see them, but I felt their presence close by.

As I mentioned earlier, they began to negatively influence my life, leading me to addiction.

And awakening in my almost uncontrollable sexual desires.Whenever I slept — a condition acquired after they stopped tormenting me during the nights — I dreamed of having sex with different types of women. When I woke up I found myself with a hard penis and many times all sperm, because in this period I was already thirteen years old and had an enviable physique, I was no longer that skinny kid and without the least beauty, all the result of the plan diabolical to lead me to a life of lust and iniquity.

I started to be harassed by prostitutes who lived in a brothel located in front of our house, on the other side of the highway, every time I passed nearby they invited me in, said that they were thirsty to take me to bed. Until that moment, I had never had sex even with the mares raised by my father.

The other boys in the neighborhood used to get into all kinds of animals ranging from pigs to donkeys, but I was repudiated by these things and I was waiting for the chance to lose my virginity to a real woman. To quench the fire of desire that burned inside me, I started to go to the banks of the stream of waters that ran there watching the whores.

There they used to bathe together with their lovers who they fucked every weekend, without the slightest ceremony, there I watched everything, masturbated in secret without anyone noticing, came, rolled my eyes at the moment of pleasure, imagining the day where I would finally put the stick in a pussy.

It was my biggest fantasy, to put my mast all inside the tail of one of those bitches, to come like a horse, to fill their hole with milk, delirious until I passed out with pleasure.

Everything I thought and wished to do was influenced by the condemned souls of my dead brother, together with the other four dark beings from hell to tempt me. What to do to escape from such a disastrous destiny? Was everything I heard from my brother killed in the war true? Or was he just an emissary of the Devil who came to make up lies, to convince me that I would be the son of the devil and thus accept the idea of committing all kinds of sin? I decided to investigate.

— Mother, whose portrait is this on the wall?

— What? The soldier's?

— Yes, who was he? Has died?

— But why this interest now, my son? This picture has been around for decades and you never gave a damn

— It's true, but now I'm curious. Tell me that story, mom?

— That one was your older brother, very rebellious by the way, it only brought us sadness and disgust. A drunk, without self-control who got lost in prostitution, gave us a lot of work in life. That God has.

— Wow, so he was really so wrong?

— My son, it may seem an inhumane attitude on my part, as a mother, but I thanked God that he was taken out of this life in the middle of life so that he can stop doing so much madness and bring us peace

— God, mother, but what a lack of feelings, after all he was your son!

— it is true, but it only brought shame, pain and disappointment, several times he was arrested, beaten by the police.

His father lived in the city police station, freeing him from jail for committing rioting at parties, bars, making trouble everywhere he went. Honestly, his death was a relief to everyone who knew him, even to us

— And how was his death, mother?

— One day he arrived here excited, said that he had been summoned to fight in the war and his father was very proud, but the conversation between them was short and the next day he traveled with one of the army platoons to face the enemies. Without any battle training it did not last even a week, days after his departure we received the news of his death, his body remained in the war field, we were unable to watch or carry out a dignified burial, his father is still moved by it today.

— Was he shot with bullets by the other soldiers?

— The Army Command only said that he died in a bomb explosion, we wanted to know more details, but nothing more we could find out about his death

— So he told me the truth ...

— As?

— It's nothing, Mom, I just thought out loud

That poor devil had spoken the truth about his unruly life, his shameful behavior while he was alive, his premature and violent death. Could it be that chatter that I had reincarnated after having lived a hundred years as one of the Demo's favorite children? Would I really have returned from hell? Well, it was something to be considered considering those five dark beings following me since I got along with people.

The ability to see the invisible, to talk to the dead and to notice what was moving in the darkness. After all, why couldn't my family members see the same things I did? What is the explanation for being such a different person from the others? It is not common for a boy my age to chat with demons or have visions of the beyond. There was really something wrong with me, I needed to investigate a little more and find out details about this previous existence and all the evils that I had committed.

Days after the disappearance of the five dark beings, on an afternoon where I decided to rest in that damn hammock, I felt the chill that announced the arrival of the condemned, they had returned from the darkness and would certainly stay there for a new conversation. It would be my chance to clarify my doubts a little more.

— Come on, get closer, I'm not afraid of you anymore!

— It's good to know that! - Completed the woman dressed in red

— I want more explanations about my past life

— Who told you that we have this information you are looking for? She answered

— José made it clear that they know a lot about me, both from this life and the past

— Smart kid, it wasn't for nothing that the Demo chose him as his son — added the one who had a super sharp hatchet in his right hand

— Come on, stop bullshit and give me the answers I need to understand all this horrible story that I came from hell, where I was chosen as the son of the Damned for having lived a life of crime and violence in the past!

— It's a long story! — Warned my dead brother

— Screw it! I still have a long time to live in this world and you are all already dead and condemned, so we are in no hurry

— Very well, come on. We are all the result of what existed in the past, that is, the God of the Universe is the Father of all spirits, whether good or mus. He created us, from Satan and his demons to every living soul on earth. When we choose to follow the guidelines of the Evil One and depart from the good, he withdraws from us and we are surrendered to the domain of evil, ending up in darkness after physical death. The Devil is fond of those who most commit atrocities, practice a greater number of evils against their fellow men, placing them prominently in his kingdom, thus, we are considered his children.

— I understand, so that's exactly what happened to me?

— That's it, you already understood everything

— But there is still something I need to know

— Which is?

— Who was I in the life before that? What was my name?

— What does it matter?

— I want to understand who exactly I was and did in previous lives

— Yes, of course, even you were recognized in the penultimate incarnation as the worst of all individuals of your time

— Oh my God. But come on, tell me at once what name I had at that time in human existence?

— First, explain how you will investigate your past in history if you don't even know how to read or write properly? — Asks the spirit with the appearance of a prostitute

— Do you know me very well and ask me such a question? Although I never inexplicably went to school I learned to read, everyone in my family admires this ability

— Stop fooling around, we did this to you, boy, everything that is now and will be later comes from our influence

— Guys, I'm going to have to wait a long time for you to give me the answer I'm looking for ?!

— Stop impatience, boy! — angered the biggest of all

They exchange glances and, seeming to be in full agreement, the dark spirit that was said to be my brother killed in the war takes the floor:

— We are not allowed to reveal to you who in fact came to be in the past life, but we can say that by the acts of madness and insanity committed against humanity he became a man immensely known as the worst of human beings and your name was engraved on the history as the one who came closest to the very likeness of satan

— What the hell, just tell me who it is!

— We cannot go any further than what we have already revealed, but it is enough for you to do your research, however, I advise you to consider the present and the future, as these two stages of life can still be changed, but your past is already it is closed and there is nothing you can do to change it

When these things were said to me, the five spirits disappeared in a haze of smoke and I woke up from that slight state of vertigo, which usually occurred whenever they approached me. I spent several days thinking about the words I heard, increasingly consumed by the immense desire to know more about the terrible person I was in my other existence.

The negative influence of the dark beings persisted in dominating me in order to return to practicing illicit, sinful acts, which would lead me to be once again worthy to return from the place where I came from, the darkness. I decided to dedicate myself to prayer and spent hours on my knees, crying out for divine mercy, but it seemed to be of no use.

Because the impure desires only increased each day to the point that on a sunny afternoon of that intense summer I had the terrible idea of staying on the banks of the stream that passed behind the puteiro where the sluts bathed, hiding me among the foliage of undergrowth. , watching all that burning with lust.

While the couples fucked nonstop I there behind the bushes I hit a handjob and with each cumshot rolled my eyes and almost passed out, but in a matter of minutes I was already hard again, wishing to be one of those males in the water to fuck those bitches. I got addicted to it to the point of every day going to watch the fuck and masturbate.

Now, in addition to drinking alcohol and smoking I became addicted to sexual immorality, my heart went completely black with so many desires, ideas, immoral thoughts that each day made me a person totally turned to darkness. The five demonic beings never left me, they dragged me with their mental power to do evil.

From the age of fourteen onwards, nothing and nobody held me back, drank, smoked, used various types of drugs, stole and even killed some who dared to challenge me. At eighteen I was arrested and spent three years behind bars, there I did not die because I became a male and put morals in place, in front of the bullies. But wait, I forgot to say when I finally put the dick in a pussy for the first time, after all this is an important detail of this story.

Second Chapter: Rape

Bianca was the only daughter of Senhora Ana, an extremely religious woman, a fervent Catholic who did not admit that her little girl even became friends with the son of sorcerers.

That old woman was one of those kind of trouble people, she hated our family, she wanted to see Capeta before her eyes and not have to see us, even from a distance.

Because of that, I decided that I was going to fuck the tomboy at any cost just to show that disgusting old woman that her daughter's pussy was not gold plated. Every time the girl with white skin, long blond hair and blue eyes went to school, she saw me sitting under a leafy tree planted in front of my house.

That was her daily commute, the only way she could get to the school where she studied, it would be impossible to avoid walking there. She always took a brief look at me, a little shy, lowered her head and smiled, when we met at the grocery store or bakery, I stared at her and the girl lacked melt with shame.

On a certain Friday night, when dawn was beginning, when my brother snored in the hammock next door, Maligno's children and I were talking about the best way for me to break into that pussy, they assured me that they would help to arouse her lust for me.

— You guys put that damned tare on me, almost irresistible, I walk to die from wanking, watching those bitches fucking in the stream with their males. Damn it, so help me get a woman off to fuck!

— I honestly do not understand how such an attractive young man has to ask the demons for help to get laid — the prostitute quipped

— Yes, after becoming a teenager I improved my physical shape, but I'm not very lucky with women

— Your father is a respected wizard here, he has prestige with his clients, everything he does works, why didn't you ask him to untie your luck for women? — Asked one of them

— Well thought out, why don't you talk to the old man?

— But why do I bother my father if I have you who can solve everything for me? Or do they not have the power to turn a woman's head to fuck with me? They are demons, servants of the Demo, they must be able to do something besides torture me as they did before, in my childhood!

— We received from our lord the power to do any kind of evil, only good we cannot do

— So do not waste time, take care to make that bitch with blue eyes completely freaked for me!

— We will, but with one condition

— What?

— Everything we do for the living is in order to gain something in return that benefits our master

— Explain it better, what do you want from me?

— You will have the chance to fuck that tomboy tomorrow, however, it will have to be on the basis of violence, by force, it is to get her all fucked up, because every time a human commits evils incited by a demon, hell shudders and the Devil rejoices

— Look here, I fought a lot against your damn influence on me, I even spent days, weeks, praying to get rid of you, but nobody up there seems to have been interested in listening to me and helping me. Therefore, I decided to give myself body and soul to you, the devil and to anyone else. What I want is a pussy to stick the stick in, I don't care about anything, it can be chipped!

— So, all set! Tomorrow she hides in that thicket on the side of the road that takes her from home to the highway, before she goes on the road you attack the tomboy, drag her into the bush, throw them on the ground and take her clothes off, then do what want and satisfy your satanic desires

— And if she screams, how do I do it?

— Cover her mouth, but don't worry, because I'll be around inciting her to want to fuck you, she will feel her pussy itching to take a dick! - promised the prostitute, always smoking her endless cigarette

— Perfect, so it will be done!

— Hit her, bite her, do all kinds of crazy things, that's the price!

— Okay, just fill me with this crazy desire to fuck and mistreat the piranha at the same time!

They disappeared after my statement, but I couldn't sleep my eyes for the rest of the morning, so the way was to jerk off to relieve the tension. After much skinning the stick with one hand, milk finally splashed from the stick and I was able to relax. However, very early in the morning I woke up with a hard cock to the point of going to fulfill my mission.

The blonde, as usual, went on her way to school, perhaps thinking that she would again see me sitting under that tree, but things that day would be quite different. As soon as the bitch turned in the curve on the narrow road, which separated the place where she lived with her mother from the paved road, I suddenly appeared, out of the bush.

— Stop there, hot!

She got scared and threw the books with notebooks on the floor, tried to turn around and run in the opposite direction, but I held her tightly by the arm

— Wait a second!

— Please let me go!

— Quiet, I told you!

After collecting her belongings that were scattered on the ground, I dragged her into the bush, after walking a hundred meters away from the dirt road I threw her on some palm leaves previously prepared for the practice of the act. I jumped on the naughty and started taking off her clothes, she kicked for not wanting to be undressed. It was a hell of a job to just take off his shirt, because despite not having greater physical strength I was quite resistant.

Okay, Dona Ana's daughter had lost her gourd, she was as little a bitch as any of the many that existed there, but the section was not yet over, a lot still had to be done. I spent about ten minutes punching the stick in that pussy, as it was the first fuck the hole was the width of my wood.

It was still possible to feel my penis curling on the walls of that soft and hot vagina, there I understood the importance of being the first to tear a pussy, only the first feels this kind of pleasure, the others who will come later will be lucky if they have the thick stick, for if it is thin, it will be as if they are going into a loose and endless ditch.

After that wave of thrusts she told him to stop, positioned himself on all fours, put his forehead against the coconut palms and raised his fleshy ass as high as possible, ordering me to first lick his alley, the entrance of his ass that flashed from horny, then suck the tight hole.

Immediately I carried out her orders, a few seconds there I was falling on that upturned ass, wanting to be fucked, licking, sucking with enormous pleasure as she moaned and rolled like a bitch in heat. The next thing to do would be to stick my sledgehammer in that ditch to break the tomb's second seal, and I did so.

The more I stuck the stick in the little hole she rolled her ass and grunted like a horny dog, I never imagined that a woman could feel in her ass the same lust that everyone feels in her pussy, but that prostitution demon felt all that through the girl's body, it only remained to be seen whether so much pleasure would remain in it afterwards. I spent even more time fucking that ass, I liked it more than the cunt because it was hotter. Tighter and more delicious, I became a fan of anal sex since that first time.

I started to feel like coming, it would be my first orgasm in an ass or pussy, but she chose another place for me to dump the milk from my dick.

— Come on, kid, come here and let me swallow your hot rod!

She got down on her knees in front of me and I remained standing, my dick prancing so hard it was, the fucking bitch put her mouth on him without worrying that seconds ago he was stuck in the girl's ass, swallowed until the end, moaning horny she started doing the back and forth, then it was I who started to punch, I fucked that throat with madness.

I took hold of her long blond hair, punched it in and out without mercy, I did it like I was fucking a pussy, like I was in that hot ass. The bitch just moaned because with a stick that big in her mouth it was impossible to say anything.

In little less than half an hour, of the almost four that we were there, I finally could not resist anymore and I came, a huge amount of sperm expired from the cock's head that seemed to fill half a glass.

She kept sucking while swallowing that creamy, hot, pasty milk, I never saw anyone enjoy drinking gala so much. After the rape was over, the demon who possessed the girl's body explained to me how things should happen from now on:

— How delightful to fuck with you, boy, it was a long time since I had experienced such pleasure, but the time has come to take that body home. Do not worry, after my departure she will remember nothing. It will all be just a dream that you will think you had while sleeping. In the meantime, she will be intimidated every time she sees you.

Because she would have been the main character in that story where she was raped, but everything in her mind is just a fantasy.

— Are you sure about that?

— Of course it is!

— It clarifies a doubt: All this lust that made her feel, both in her pussy and in her ass, the crazy desire to swallow my cock, will everything remain in her body after your departure?

— Only if I want to give her all these things

— So please, because a woman who doesn't have these sexual qualities can't consider herself good in bed, we'll make up for what we take from her by giving her such qualities

— Okay, so it will be done, I will make her a bitch

— Thanks, demon, turn her into a super horny bitch, that the desire to suck, gives her ass and pussy to burn inside her day and night

— You want to fuck her again, aren't you, you bastard?

— Yes, but this time I want it to be a clean and fair fuck, with her even wanting to fuck me and not with a demon inside her

— Okay, whatever you want

After dressing up and collecting her school supplies, the dark spirit leads the girl home, arriving there she finds her mother in the kitchen making lunch, the teenager goes silent and the woman finds her behavior strange

— Bianca, my daughter, did something happen at school?

— No, mom, why?

— You look weird today ...

— What do you mean, stranger?

— Every day when you get home from school you come here, we talk and you go right through the pots, always starving, today you went straight to your room, you didn't even talk to me

— Sorry, mom, I just don't feel very well today

— What are you feeling, any pain or discomfort?

— Mother, please, after I rest and feel better we talk, okay?

— Okay, I'll make tea for you when you wake up

The demon who had taken possession of the girl did not know the exact relationship between mother and daughter, so she ended up getting in the way, but managed to get around the situation.

After taking a shower, cleaning the girl's private parts led him to the bedroom, laying her on the bed where he withdrew from the body, throwing a heavy sleep on it.

Meanwhile, not far from there, I was anxiously awaiting the return of the dark spirit with the latest news about Bianca, which soon happened, because suddenly a type of smoke appeared before my eyes and I could see that evil being coming towards me, a terrible odor of sulfur washed over me

— How were things over there, demon?

— Everything went as planned

— So the old woman didn't suspect anything, do you still think you have a gourd daughter?

— Worse than that, old sucker!

The spirit from the darkness gave me this answer while settling in some corner, sat in an old chair that existed in the place, crossed his legs and continued to smoke that damn cigarette that never came to an end.

We spent hours talking and I had the opportunity to learn more about the history of those five demons.

— To start, boy, stop calling us dark spirits or demons, agreed?

— And I'm going to call them, how? Do you happen to have a proper name like João, Maria, Pedro ...?

— You can bet it is, but it is not similar to the names of the living

— There are, I understand, are names used by the dead, but since when does a soul or spirit still have a name?

— Boy, you don't know a third of things about the spirit world!

— Of course not, how would I know something about the other side if I have never been there?

— But, as we already told you, you have been in our world several times, you just don't remember

— I think this is foolish, of what use is the reincarnation of the human soul if you forget everything that you lived in previous lives?

How will you be able to correct the mistakes made in the past if you remember nothing in the present?

— Superior decisions should not be discussed

— We cannot remain inert while God or the Devil plays back and forth with us

— The return of the soul to this plane is necessary for the evolution of the human race to occur, because the Creator of the Universe finished Creation after the seven days and since then we have been a repetition of existences in this world

— Are you trying to convince me that the current generation is formed by the same souls that existed at the beginning of Creation? Did the people who died in the Flood reincarnate from Noah's descendants and from there everything is repeated?

She smiles and continues with her explanations:

— This is exactly how things happen, all due to the action of the power of sin that extinguished the permanent life of human beings on earth, after our master convinced the first couple to practice disobedience their kingdom was established in this world, now, everything what is born must inevitably die and then return to life

— What a bitch this is! Is it the same with animals?

— Without a doubt, even with the plants. Everything in nature is renewed, redone!

— How many existences have you had?

— Me, several, they too

— After the disembodied soul remembers all its previous existences or only the last?

— We remember every detail of all previous lives, nothing is covered up in our eyes, we are even able to review what we were and practice good or bad

— What the fuck, so I just can't remember who I was before that incarnation because I'm stuck with that body?

— Exactly! In fact, we have both had an intimate involvement in one of our past lives, we live as husband and wife

— Fuck, now I understand why you fucked me so horny!

— That's right, boy, you were one of my best lovers!

— And how did it end like this, like a demon of prostitution?

— First, I want you to stop calling me a demon again!

— Sorry, what should I call you?

— Because my last existence in this mortal world was turned to promiscuity, sexual immorality and various types of crimes, Satan was pleased with me to the point of putting me in the air of his women, my new name is “Pomba-Gira” which means "Queen of Whores"

— Credo, what a horrible thing!

— I don't think, only he gave me such a title

— And does he let you out of hell and walk around?

If we were lovers in the past, doesn't he feel jealous? After all, that kind of feeling comes from him

— He has the power to see through our eyes and hear through our ears, so he knows everything

— Understand. So is he seeing and listening to us right now?

— Completely!

Third Chapter: The Darkness

My conversation with the Queen — the way I started to treat the demon of immorality — was very productive and enlightening, with her I understood how things work in the spiritual world although, as she explained to me, I already knew about everything she said, however it was impossible to remember being embodied in physical matter.

Through her I was also aware that Bianca, the raped teenager, woke up from sleep hours later without remembering anything that had happened to her and not even her two little holes or throat were sore, because the Queen took care that this did not happen, that way she she wouldn't complain to her mother and she wouldn't take her to the doctor.

In the following weeks we continued to use and abuse the body of the hot tomboy without her realizing it, the Queen incorporated her and we fucked her until my cock spit out milk. But little by little I got tired of always fucking the same woman. and my new friend started to have other bodies, improving the sex routine.

We started to practice all kinds of sexual immorality, it entered the bodies of girls, married or single adult women, elderly people, even in gays I stuck the stick in the ass. I became lost in every way, the other four dark spirits that tormented me at first were absent for some time, the Queen told me that they were on other missions at the behest of the Demo.

Her husband, but suddenly one day they returned to report that the Devil was very satisfied with the results obtained by his wife. The mission of the five was to transform myself into an extremely evil being to the point of being rejected by God and thus losing the chance to die when taken to heaven, because he wanted me by his side.

Which the Queen was managing to do with much success. However, the new order given directly by the leader of the dark spirits was to increase the dose. The four returned with the mission to further worsen my state of moral calamity, by going beyond being a slave to prostitution, becoming a complete delinquent.

The demon who introduced himself to me as Joseph, who in the previous life was my father's son and my older brother, was tasked with giving me the dexterity to wield a firearm. The one with a very sharp hatchet in my right hand would give me agility in using all kinds of cutting weapons.

And the big man with long hands that used to crush my testicles as a child would give me physical strength to fight any opponent hand to hand. So it was and at the age of twenty I became a criminal without limits. The first step my parents took was to expel me from home, then I was arrested for murder, armed robbery, drug trafficking and many other heinous crimes.

I got a fifteen-year sentence in a closed regime, but the dark ones helped me and I got out of jail through the front door with the conviction forgiven by justice. The demons took possession of the judge's body and the latter issued my Release Permit, I was only a week behind bars.

In addition to being released, I still had my name removed from the police files, that is, there would be nothing against me. Aware that I could count on the help of hell, I started to commit worse crimes, I lost count of how many people I killed. When I was twenty-five years old I was invited by the father of darkness to visit his kingdom.

I was transferred in spirit to the darkness, there I could see with the eyes of the soul how tremendous the suffering of those who die far from God is tremendous, there is only darkness wherever you go, on all sides you can hear moans, screams and gnashing of teeth. I remembered what is written in the Holy Scriptures about the fate of those who reject salvation.

And whose names are not written in the Book of the Lamb: ***"I saw thrones; and they sat on them, and they were given the power to judge; and I saw the souls of those who were beheaded by the testimony of Jesus, by the word of God, who did not worship the beast or its image, did not receive the mark on their foreheads or in their hands; and lived, reigned with Christ for a thousand years.***

But the other dead did not live again, until the thousand years were over. This is the first resurrection. Blessed and holy is he who has a part in the first resurrection; the second death has no power over these; but they will be priests of God and of Christ, and will reign with him a thousand years, when the thousand years are over, Satan will be released from his prison. He will deceive the nations that are on the four corners of the earth, Gog and Magog, whose number is like the sand of the sea. To gather them in battle, they went up over the width of the land, and surrounded the camp of the saints.

Also the beloved city; and fire came down from God out of heaven and devoured them. The devil, who deceived them, was cast into the lake of fire and brimstone, where the beast and the false prophet are; and day and night they will be tormented forever and ever.

I saw a great white throne, and the one that sat on it, from whose presence the earth and the sky fled; and no place was found for them. And I saw the dead, great and small, who were before God, and the books were opened; and another book was opened, which is the book of life. And the dead were judged by the things that were written in the books, according to their works.

The dead gave the sea that was in it; death and hell gave up the dead in them; and each was judged according to his works. Death and hell were cast into the lake of fire. This is the second death. He who was not found written in the book of life was thrown into the lake of fire. " Revelation 20: 4-15

I walked along paths that at one time were narrow, on others wide, slippery, covered in mud, mud, totally wet and dirty. Condemned souls live chained to poles, hanging upside down, naked, whipped, humiliated, suffering from pity. Seeing all that made me wonder if the direction I went there was ideal for me.

Whether I would want to end up like those miserable creatures or choose to go up to the Celestial Kingdom. I was called to appear before the prince of darkness to receive some kind of honor from him, but I was still unsure whether I would accept such a gift. We walked for at least half an hour until we saw the palace of the damned, The Queen.

Along with the other demons followed side by side with me, like an escort, around hundreds of armed beings with pointed spears, dressed as warriors ready for battle, possessed on the back were two huge wings that flew from side to side.

His eyes were red, they smoked like flames of fire, his chest carried something with the appearance of an impenetrable cuirass, a shiny helmet on his head, a yellowish vapor came out of his mouth, whose stench was similar to sulfur. In fact, everything there had this unpleasant odor, so I could understand why this horrible smell in the five shadows.

Finally we arrived in front of the Demo's amazing castle and were told that he was waiting for us in his real space, the Queen went ahead with the other demonic beings while I accompanied them escorted by two demons dressed as guards with their weapons in fists, the The place was dark, chilling.

It seems strange to say that it gives chills if at that moment I was in the spirit there, however, it is very important to remember that our senses such as pain, fear, joy and sadness, despair or dread, as well as everything that our bodies feel comes from soul and not his own, hence it becomes necessary for us to know how to avoid going to the lower regions of the earth.

Yes, because for those who do not know, hell really exists and is in the central part of this immense planet, however, it is a place totally invisible to the human eye and this is the answer for skeptics, the followers of modern science where everything that is denied is denied. it is related to the spiritual, to materialists who only believe in what can be touched.

With each step taken a new horror scene to be seen and heard, in the wide hall of the palace of horrors where we passed there were countless compartments, within which we saw the souls of people — formerly distinguished in the outside world — chained, trapped by the feet and hands, some with iron rings around the neck, the scene was really macabre.

Satan is a great collector of souls, especially those on earth who have become important within world society, who commit evils against the less fortunate, deceive, steal, kill, corrupt, accumulate material goods, earthly riches, ambitious to the extreme, these very catch your eye.

I saw the souls of movie and television celebrities, actors, actresses, great and renowned scientists, journalists, doctors, lawyers, judges, corrupt politicians, pedophile priests, evangelical pastors who sold the Gospel and enriched themselves at the expense of the faith of others ... They were all there because the sin was great against their fellow men.

There was a sign nailed to the top of the cells where they paid their feathers, on it was written the name of each of them, describing their origins, who they were, why they were there, in large and clearly visible letters, for this reason I could identify them easily. These people considered themselves powerful because of their wealth, now they were in agony of pain.

His relatives certainly believed that they would all be resting in heaven — the Catholic religion teaches in its doctrine about death that everyone goes straight to heaven when they disincarnate, but what idiocy! — However, there were your loved ones burning in the flames of hell, because one thing is certain,

In the Kingdom of God these types of people will not enter, at the end of the wide corridor, with chains on both sides, we turned to the right towards the place where the one who was waiting for us was to be aware of our arrival in his kingdom. Finally we were face to face with the Demo, we were allowed to address him and the Queen introduced me to the damn.

— As requested, here is the one that your majesty has entrusted us with bringing here

He got up from his seat, dressed in a black suit, a pair of huge horns in place of his ears, his nose was similar to that of a giant pig, a large solid gold ring was attached to him, the individual should measure about two meters or more, his hands were huge as were the nails on his long fingers, his feet were like those of a duck and his gaze smoldering flames.

When speaking the whole kingdom shuddered and his subjects bowed to worship him, however, I remained standing, despite the two armed beings positioned beside me ordering me to humble myself in the presence of the wicked one, however, I insistently refused to obey such an order, at that moment, I would not be able to explain why I refused to worship him.

Being a king in his own spiritual realm, but today I understand the reasons for my bold attitude. After much insistence on the part of the two thugs for me to kneel, he interferes in my favor:

— Leave him alone!

The order is immediately obeyed

You remain the same stubborn and rebellious as always, my son, hasn't changed at all since he decided to leave and reincarnate up there!

Interesting how what the Queen had told me about the soul easily remembering all her past lives was really true, when I heard the words of the one who said my spiritual father came to mind all my story before my last incarnation, leading me to remember every detail of that place.

— Now you are watching this environment more closely, aren't you? Well, yes, I had closed his mind so that he would not remember his own home, however, now I allow him that right, because I was very proud of everything he has done up there.

After looking around and making sure of every detail I realized that really what the Queen and the other four dark beings told me was true. She and her cronies went to the Demo's throne and stood beside him, he held out his hands to me, calling me to join them in that false role of family.

However once again I refused to be part of that theater, after all, since when Satan wastes his time showing affection for someone, he being the worst enemy of humanity, of God, of the most important work of his hands which is the family, for what reason was he doing that ridiculous scene, landing like a father surrounded by his wife and children?

Tremendous clowning! — I thought — if I was called there to contemplate such a comic moment, I would immediately return from where I came. However, aware of my thoughts, he soon cried out in that horrible demon voice.

— Don't you dare turn your back on me again, my boy!

I have been patient in the extreme with his acts of rebellion, but now I have reached my limit.

I am determined to punish him severely if I take just one more step towards the exit of this castle, understand? I was already facing the immense corridor, however, standing on that almost infinite red carpet, in front of the two giant guards who placed their crossed arms on my chest. To keep me from going ahead. Upon hearing such threatening words, I turned to that king and gave him an answer in line with his arrogance:

— Don't be so arrogant as to think that you can intimidate me with your threats, neither with this horrible appearance of a giant pig or with anything else that wants to make me fear you!

— You insolent, how dare you challenge me like that?

— I already said that I have no fear in the face of your threats!

— Respect your father, he is not just anybody to address him that way! - The Queen roared

— And who do you think it is to give me such an order?

I wish I never asked such a question, because the answer greatly intrigued and disturbed my conscience to discover the worst of all the mistakes already practiced in my few years of existence.

— She's your mother, you asshole!

Be astonished by the situation, asking me what the hell was going on with me, that dark spirit manifested itself before me claiming to be Demo's wife, then it got me horny. Then she proposed to incarnate in the bodies of several women so that I could have her sexually, she said that in one of her incarnations we had an affair, we fell in love with each other, she became my wife.

Now I discover that in the spiritual world she was always my mother? Most Holy Mary, but what madness! — I thought

— Were you surprised, son? Yes, we are your parents here in the world of darkness and for that reason you owe us respect!

— Dad, let me give a correction to that asshole? — Asks one of the demons

— Nothing like that, don't get involved in this subject!

— What do you want, you muggles, do you think you can face me?

— Kid, do not forget that the courage, strength and ability you have comes from us, just an order given by our father and you were already, will not be anyone else!

— Stop this discussion without a future, a kingdom that fights among itself will be defeated, we are all the same family, I order you to respect each other! — The king of darkness raged

— Look here, you two, I want to return immediately to my body up there, I have been down here for a long time and he could die!

— What an idiot, would you rather go back to live in that miserable little life of crime than be with us in that kingdom that you too belong to?

— You bet!

— Well know that I will not allow you to return, your place is here beside us!

— If I already managed to get out of this damn hell and started a new existence on earth.

Then there must be a way to return without it depending on you, your pig snout!

— Insolent, guards, trap that bastard in the worst hole in this kingdom!

— Calm down, my king, he's our son!

— Damn it, it's time to teach this kid who gives the orders here!

I was savagely grabbed by the two thugs who led me to one of the many moats on the outside of the palace, then thrown there inside the trapdoor covered by a steel screen over it, with a lot of rotten mud that covered me up to the neck, I passed several weeks stuck on that drug according to my own count.

I worried all the time about what state my physical body could be up there, because I left him in that bed in a cheap hotel in the Urubu slum, I feared that someone would enter there, see me out and take the body to the hospital. If the doctors were unable to revive me, I would be considered dead, buried as destitute, that would be the end of the bite.

Would remain locked in the drug of that grave for as long as the Demo determined and then I would return to the haunted castle forever, damn demons! They intended to keep me imprisoned in that drug of darkness, to take away my freedom, to cancel the new existence that I acquired in some way, but I would not allow such a thing.

Needed to discover how I returned to the world of the living and reincarnated, was it God who ordered the Devil to allow this new life? Or do the demons have the power to reincarnate on their own without the Father of spirits interfering in the process?

Had no answers to such questions, so I needed to get out of there as soon as possible to find out what to do to get up and resume my life. If I cried out to the Father of Lights, would he send an angel to help me? Another unfortunate question without answers that would help me solve such a problem.

The solution was to wait for the pig's snout to send his subordinates to rescue me from that filthy hole, full of rotting mud. It did not rain there, the light of the sou did not reach us, but there was a waterfall of filth running steadily into the ditches, it wasn't just me who was almost drowned in those pits, many other souls were struggling there.

But they certainly had no hope of being taken out of there at any time. As the son of the damn Demo, my punishment would be limited, it was just a corrective, certainly the order for my release would soon be given. However, in the meantime, my suffering increased the house where the mud rose inside the ditch.

Being drained from a type of waterfall coming from a crust located in the highest part of the place where we were trapped. I was startled to hear dreadful screams coming from one of the prisoners who were approaching me. Some brutes put their pointed spears at the poor devils who could not defend themselves from the attacks.

Because the space was too small to dodge, so they were exposed to all kinds of torture. The whole time I was standing and with mud at the height of my neck we could hardly breathe, seeing such cruelty I wondered if I would not be next. The rest of the prisoners were tortured in different ways, they just screamed without any means of getting rid of the fetters.

That bound them, each one paid there what they owed. Suddenly two of the ugly animals approached, stopped talking to each other, giving the impression that they were deciding what to do against me. I took them seriously, doubting whether they would dare torment their master's son with his pointed spears, but I struggled with my concepts.

Because while they were talking they seemed to have been mentally ordered to punish me. Soon they went to the pit where I was and without wasting time started attacking me with their weapons Believe me if you want, but people outside the physical body continue to feel the same pains, at that moment I couldn't help screaming.

Every time the sharp points of their weapons seemed to pierce me, even if I was in spirit. In reality everything seems to be real, but deep down it is illusory, as if it were in a dream, but it hurts to tape! Being there, standing and attached to the steel screen placed at the top of the filthy hole where they put me, by the steel chains.

I had to endure the martyrdom caused by those two bastards. My greatest hatred was not against them, but against the bastard who ordered my punishment, I swore to myself that I would take revenge. Maybe I wouldn't have enough power to confront the dark king or his army, but I could do a lot of damage in that miserable kingdom.

Well, at least I would try. Then they walked away, letting me rest and in this space of time I had the idea of seeking help from the Father of lights, through a brief prayer. So, I started talking to our Creator in thought, believing that he was heard, who knows somehow my pleas would be answered, he could send help, rescue me from the clutches of the evil one.

Restore my life on earth, allow my return to the body that he had somehow given me. I sought refuge in himself, trapped in that darkness, for I remembered that in the Holy Scriptures it is written:

"Where will I go from your spirit, or where will I flee from your face? If you go up to heaven, there you are; if I make my bed in hell, behold, you are there too. If I take the wings of the morning, if I live at the ends of the sea, your hand will guide me there and your right hand will sustain me.

If I say: Surely the darkness will cover me; then the night will be light around me. Even darkness does not cover me from you; but the night shines like the day; darkness and light are the same for you" Psalm 139: 7-12

Later, I was removed from the hole where I was confined long enough to feel my strength wane, which I admired a lot, since it was not in my body. I was taken to a freshwater spring where I was told to bathe and clean the filthy mud that covered me from head to toe, then they took me in new clothes to the presence of the pig snout that insisted on saying my father.

After again rejecting his demands, it was determined that they would arrest me next to a wooden post. I was tied by strong chains that ran from my legs to my chest, a lot of dry wood was placed around me and they lit a fire whose fire licked me whole. I could feel the heat melting into an extraordinary pain, my terrifying screams were lost in an intense echo reflected in the dirty walls, filled with mud from that cursed place. In a blink of an eye that despair ceased because everything disappeared before my eyes.

The fire was gone, I was no longer attached to the pole and I was in no pain. Another scenario was formed, now the soldiers of evil arrested me with hard bonds by the feet, I was positioned upside down and beaten by punches and kicks for several hours.

Whenever I lost consciousness I received a bucket of water in my face and woke up to yet another wave of beating, it seemed to last forever. Finally, one of the five dark spirits who came to me as a boy approached me, was the one who carried his inseparable, very sharp hatchet.

The bastard surrounded me for a few seconds, as he was facing his filthy ground, it was difficult to face him in the face, but by the gun he carried in his right hand and his legs I could identify him perfectly, asking for his help, but he if he refused to help me, he laughed a lot to ridicule my miserable state.

— Look at Dad's wayward little boy, asking for mercy! Where's that bullshit, sucker? Where's your arrogance?

— Dude, get me out of here, let me go!

— Fuck you shit, I didn't come here to set you free, but to take your head off with my gun!

When he said that he passed his hatchet around my neck and while my head rolled on the floor my eyes could see and my ears heard his ironic laughter that echoed inside that damn cell.

Suddenly everything went dark, but within a few seconds my vision lit up, I was transported to other macabre scenarios. First I found myself lying under a giant guillotine.

Two parts made of steel held me by the neck and both hands, suddenly I heard a noise as if something was falling from the top, it was the sharp blade coming towards me. The desperation to know that in a few seconds my head would be separated from my body again made me shiver.

Terrified, I wanted to get out of there, but it was impossible to do, I was helpless, completely trapped and helpless, I once again felt that bitter taste of being divided into two parts. Then, stuck to a chair, my nails were pulled out, my eyes were leaked, I was burned with smoldering embers.

My feet and hands were broken with hammering ...Marious forms of martyrdom have been thrown at me because of my decision not to abide by the Demo's ordinances within his own realm, rebelling me definitively against his authority. Finally, they took me back to the presence of the Evil One who ordered the punishment he applied to me to cease.

Due to my insubordination, the Queen and the other dark ones remained standing beside the throne of the pig's snout, while giving me the usual scolding, then transported in spirit throughout the kingdom, showing me everything. He never gave up on having me by his side, he seemed to want to give me the command of everything there.

Although in reality we were not his real children, because the Devil cannot have sex or generate lives, he, together with his fallen angels, have no physical body and for that to be able to do this it is necessary to act like the Queen, to possess the body of someone alive. After such a walk through the high and low parts of hell I saw so much horror that I could not understand how at some point in my existence I could want to live there with the demons, the number of lost souls is immense.

It seems to be another world in the center of the earth , and they are all always moaning, screaming, cursing God for their pain, but this is pure ignorance, after all, we are responsible for our actions and not him, before I went to hell I got everything done, as I mentioned, but I don't blame anyone for that.

Satan carried me into darkness and held me captive for a long time — well, at least I thought so — and I was punished for my rebellion. However, what I did was to humble myself in the presence of God and ask him to somehow get rid of those bonds, I didn't wait long to receive the answer, the pig's snout decided to order my release. Those poor souls were condemned for their own fault.

After walking through the high and low parts of the darkness, after seeing close up the suffering of so many lost people and understanding what results from the bad decisions we made in life while we lived on earth, Demo transported me again to the palace, where they were reunited the Queen and the other dark spirits.

There I was placed in a narrow sabbath in which they demanded an immediate decision making, they wanted me to position myself in favor or not of remaining in the kingdom of darkness, giving up life up there, letting the body of my new existence die, however , he was not at all determined to give up what he had received from God. Dessa forma, eles muito esbravejaram, apresentaram-me suas ameaças, dando-me um ultimato como resultado da minha opção em recusar a oferta de satanás:

— Understand now that if you choose to return to live among mortals you will no longer be able to count on our total protection.

Finding himself in dire straits, he will have to fend for himself to escape the persecutions of his enemies, prisons and everything that comes against his life, as we will turn our backs on them — warned Demo

— And there is another detail, my son, from the moment when the whole hell turns its back on us, it will become your enemy, we will order you to be pursued by the worst of our subjects who will dominate the minds of humans with the intention of pursuing you, seeking his death twenty-four hours until at last he is plucked from his body and returns here, but he will not be received as a prince of darkness, but as one of those many doomed souls — completed the Queen

— No problem, I accept to take the risk as long as they allow me to return

— Very well, — concluded the king of darkness — so be it! From now on this kingdom will not receive you again as a son, prince and heir, but we will be your enemies until the end of its existence in the world of mortals. After the death of your physical body, we will launch you into the deepest pit that will be prepared exclusively for you. When you wake up you will not remember anything you saw, heard or lived here, however we will fulfill everything we have just announced!

Having said these words, he held out his hand in my direction and I could hear a tremendous explosion, followed by a terrible smoke with an unbearable sulfur smell. fajuta where I was before I was taken by demons to hell. The most interesting thing is that the hands of the old clock, hanging on the wall of the room, seemed to have stopped all the time that I was traveling in spirit through the dense darkness.

Or else everything had happened in just a few minutes, because it was still the end of the same dawn , the same day, month and year when they came to pick me up there. In fact, as I was promised at that moment, I remembered nothing, for mine it seems to have been a dream, only years later this whole story came to mind.

Before my trip to the lower regions of the earth to know the most terrible part of the spiritual world, I was possessed by the forces of evil and committed many evils. I raped, killed, stole, practiced absurd things that I still regret today, remaining unpunished, but the time had come to give an account for my actions, hell had promised that he would pursue me.

Stay on my trail until I completely destroyed myself, so he started to act as soon as possible so that his threats were properly fulfilled. From there demons were sent to awaken in my enemies the desire for revenge so that the worst could happen to me, as soon as I woke up with time to breathe through my body.

I saw the door being broken open, the place was invaded by armed police to the teeth that overwhelmed me by surprise. From there I was taken to the presence of an official who announced my arrest in compliance with a court order expelled by a judge, it turns out that I always got rid of the various crimes committed against society because the Queen.

Together with her subjects, dominated the minds of the defenders of the law to order my release. I never spent twenty-four hours in a police cell, then the order came for me to be released. That was how I never paid a penalty after committing all the countless atrocities against innocent people, but from that moment on, without the protection of evil.

Everything would be demanded of me. Each of my crimes, the acts of violence, the injustices, the pain that I made many families feel when they lost their loved ones ... They would be paid. Days after my arrest, I appeared before the judge at the hearing where I would be tried for my crimes, by a popular jury, where the final verdict was as guilty.

The maximum penalty established in accordance with the law was thirty years of imprisonment in a closed regime, during the trial there were dozens of people, most of them relatives of the victims killed by me, as well as some of those who were in some way victimized by my crimes that were rooting for my immediate conviction.

As soon as I entered the room I looked around to see if my family members were present, but none of them attended, but I understood your reasons, after all, who would want to be connected to a criminal of the highest kind like me? After the conclusion of the trial, being escorted to a maximum security prison.

I still took one last look outside the Court to try to see my parents or siblings and this time I was lucky because I saw my mother in the distance, she was supported by one of my sisters, exactly the youngest of them who I raped several times, which touched me very much to know that her presence there meant her forgiveness.

Our mother was crying over my misfortune, I could see this detail that moved me a lot, but my other brothers and dad did not show their faces ashamed. They took me to the detention center about ten kilometers away from the city, during the whole trip I wondered what would become of me after I found myself among other criminals of the worst kind.

Especially those with whom I had feuds, as many of them had strife with me, others lost relatives, friends or stole precious goods from them. I had been a terror in the lives of the other bandits, the bus that took us to that place stopped, making me aware that we had arrived, so I became more and more apprehensive.

Because it was time to prepare for the worst. They introduced me into the corridor, I received a yellow suit, towels and other belongings, pushed me into cell number 365 where there were already two more inmates, I was baptized in 2233, that would be my name thereafter as a condemned person. .

Everyone knew my story, awaited the arrival of the individual who spread fear and terror across the state without ever being arrested once, they believed they had a part with the Devil. Worst of all, they did not even imagine their suspicions to be true, but now the situation was different because they had lost their protection from darkness.

I was exposed, vulnerable, they could even kill me if they wanted to, but I didn't even remember all these details, the two bad guys looked at me burning with hatred, making plans against me. There were three beds housed in that cramped cell, measuring around six square meters, which required us to be very close to each other.

Increasing the possibility of a sudden attack, the hours passed through a strong tension between us, they stared at me all the time and I seriously retaliated, showing courage. At one point, I saw the wall behind them go black, opening a crack from which the demon Joseph came out along with another darkness.

They laughed at me sarcastically, invaded the bodies of the detainees, attacked me with the fury of hell in an attempt to kill me, one of them punched me hard in the stomach and fell. The other kicked my face that bled my nose, a sequence of kicks and kicks started, lasting for almost an hour, I tried to defend myself.

I retaliated a few times, but my little physical strength did nothing to prevent the beating. Before, no bastard would be able to do that to me because he had the strength of a giant. However, there I was without any defense, because Satan took from me the speed, the strength, the agility he received.

It was just a chicken without any dexterity that would lead me to confront the height with those cursed demons. While they beat me, they found grace, mocked, criticized my shameful state, but I understood nothing. His eyes were on fire, his teeth were gnarled, he was thirsty for death on their faces.

But it seems that it was not yet my time, so they could do nothing but apply a corrective, then they went back into darkness through the same crack in the wall, leaving the two detainees unaware of what happened there. I was all broken, injured, bleeding a lot due to the beating suffered at the hands of the damned.

My eyes were immensely swollen that I could barely see. Because of my screams the other prisoners woke up and started to hit the bars, causing a lot of noise in the cell corridor. This caught the attention of jailers who went to see what had happened, however it took too long to take this initiative.

Allowing the scoundrels to break me all over. In fact, I even believe that they took time on purpose, as they already expected the other inmates to beat me up, everything was planned. What they did not imagine was that demons sent from hell would lend a hand to my cellmates.

For they still saw me as that goodwill criminal, invincible, never defeated before, it turns out that I had lost all my agility since I came back from the darkness, I was devoid of such defenses. With the arrival of the jailers, the two cellmates were awakened, astonished to realize what they had done to me.

Without understanding anything, they swore innocence to the guards who cared little for their actions against me. Get out on a stretcher to the infirmary to treat the injuries. As I looked up at one of those who took me lying on that bed, I saw the fire of hell burning in his eyes.

When they arrived at the destination, everyone there was also possessed by the evil spirits, Satan dominated each one of them. The nurse sewed my wounds, treated the bruises without saying anything. I saw other demons hovering around, they seemed to take care of everything there, their influences on the lives of those people were notorious.

All of that terrified me, asking what those beings from the other world could be, because I had forgotten who it was. I was surprised by all that. Since opening the crack in the wall, seeing them own the two inmates who beat me, the instant they abandoned their bodies. To be able to see them hanging around the infirmary ... all that was at least bizarre. Nor could he comment on what he saw with the others present at the site because they seemed to be possessed by a demonic force, it would be a waste of time.

Back in the cell, I started to worry again about the two thugs who beat me, even though until that moment I was still confused about the current events, because I couldn't remember the events that happened in the past, when I went down to hell.

In reality, he did not even remember living with the Queen, Joseph and the other dark spirits in childhood, adolescence, as well as part of youth. I had only vague memories of the insane acts committed at the time I lived as a delinquent, so I was satisfied with the conviction in order to pay for my crimes.

In the weeks that I spent locked up without even being able to walk properly, going to do my needs with great difficulty, I had nights of intense nightmares, where I saw myself walking through the darkness, facing all kinds of demons, being tortured by them. They were small memories of my descent into hell, kept in my memory.

Satan may even erase our memories, but the human mind has the power to recover and that was exactly what was happening to me, little by little everything that was hidden was revealing itself, taking shape, making what was hidden return to have form, to be understood.

Sometimes these memories came in the form of dreams, at other times they seemed real, the demons sent from the darkness manifested themselves almost instantly before my frightened eyes, they appeared standing in the corner of the cell, sitting on the beds beside the other prisoners, they walked towards back and forth, impatient as if awaiting an order. Only I saw them, heard them and witnessed their concerns, however, in addition to almost frightening me with their horrible appearances.

They said nothing or did nothing. They did not attack me anymore, nor did they touch me as in the days when they tormented me, now they just stayed around day and night without ceasing, that was distressing, gradually I started to get used to that situation.

I didn't really understand why I could see hell itself opening up, sending its demons to be there beside me, but I knew that there must be some explanation. Do they do nothing wrong against me because I am like this, all broken? What will you do when you are healed? — Aske.

Still in a deplorable state after the beating taken by the cell partners, dominated by the darkness coming directly from hell, bandaged by the rib region, on the head and arm in the plaster, I received my food on a tray right there because I was unable to go to the cafeteria . But weeks later, when I found myself restored, I went to the place.

While I was in line, the other guys were staring at me and gossiping about each other about me. Surely they would be planning something against me, it got worse when I looked around and saw more demons circling around, I knew that things would not end well. I took the tray of food, sat down at the table.

Started to eat without taking my eyes off the other inmates, positioned myself with my back to the wall to avoid any surprise attack, could barely swallow the food without making a lump in my throat. The table where I sat had more empty chairs, three big ones approached. They sat down, started to talk and at one point the biggest one invented a schism with each other, dropped his hands heavily on the table that dropped all our trays on the floor, then looked at me, asking if I had bothered with his attitude.

I noticed his intentions and remained silent, I remained silent, I didn't do anything or mention even a syllable, we were all standing, no one dared to say something to the giant over two meters tall who breathed threats and showed that he wanted only one reason to grind my body with his huge hands. I was not stupid and followed the example of others, I kept silent.

However, his intent was to crush me, he felt an inexplicable hatred for me, that's when I looked at his reddish gaze, they flared, it was once again the power of hell that was working against me through the other prisoners. I didn't remember, but the Demo swore that he would chase me until I took my soul from the body where I chose to live.

In the blink of an eye, the thugs dominated by the demons that were present in the place raised the table in my direction, almost hitting me in case I had not been agile in dodging. Angered and full of rage he threw himself at me for a choke, but a loud voice ordered him to stop.

— Enough! We don't want him to die so easily, take him to the torture room!

The giant with long hands moves away and two other big guys hold my arms in tugs, I am taken to the place mentioned by the voice from beyond that could be heard, however, no one could see, it certainly came straight from the realm of the dead, it was that snout pork with duck feet who gave such an order. Arriving in that room, I was tied to a chair, then one of the convicts appears with a suitcase full of tools. They were accessories used by jailers in the prison unit to torture prisoners of justice until they opened their mouths. In order to force them to reveal secrets that would help them locate and arrest other crime bosses.

However, there it would be used to pluck my skin at the will of the demons that fulfilled the determination of their Main Man. I spent at least three or four hours, being tortured in cold blood by the dark spirit embodied in that man.

They pulled out my toenails and hands, one after the other, I even lost the strength to scream, passed out and was woken up several times. That act of pure evil was similar to the situation experienced in my visions, when the Devil caused me to be transported to various types of places and suffered countless martyrdoms.

However, the difference there is that the scenarios would not change, they would not be just illusory flashes to frighten my soul, the pain felt would not disappear or the wounds would heal quickly. After extracting the nails, they tied me upside down by a strong rope, going on to beat my face, the head, punched my stomach.

I took kicks, punched every possible part of my body, leaving me ground. The final goal would be my death in a slow and painful way, but as if by a miracle they stopped beating me. Two of them untied my feet and I fell from the top of my face on the coarse floor of that scrotum.

There they left me stretched, bleeding, almost lifeless, I extinguished my senses due to feeling immense pain, my carnal eyes closed, but those of the soul remained open, being able to see the wall open again, allowing the entrance of an evil being, that one A woman dressed as a harlot, whose clothes were red and immoral, approached me.

Fourth Chapter - Betrayal

The queen, wife of the king of darkness, decided to intervene in my state of calamity, preventing the dark beings from continuing torture until my death, she was the one who ordered the beating to stop. Certainly Demo should have been aware of his intervention or he would have rebelled against the father of darkness, which would be a very serious matter. As soon as it touched my almost broken body, I felt a strong relief, it was as if a miracle happened, the pain stopped, all the bruises disappeared, the wounds were closed and the bones were connected. But that only came to me after I woke up from that blackout that looked more like a trance, a vision.

— When you wake up your whole body will be restored, healed. Get up from this place, go to your cell, lie down and rest. Do not seek revenge against your oppressors, because they were used by the children of darkness, they are the ones who arouse hatred, anger and the desire to kill in men. When you wake up everything will be as before, the other inmates will not even remember what happened, do not comment anything.

— Why are you helping me? Did the father of demons send you?

— Do not ask difficult questions to answer, no matter if I came by his determination or on my own. Now do everything as I said.

I did as I was told, as soon as I left that brief faint I realized that everything in me was normal, nothing broken or any symptoms of beating.

Even my toenails and hands were in place. I didn't know if demons had healing power. But I later read in the Holy Bible that God would give them that gift, God will give Satan the power to work various types of prodigies on the surface, among human beings to confuse them and thus migrate the faith they may have had in Creator. And this time has come, many false prophets are already in this world performing healings, feats in the name of Christ.

That day I was healed by the miraculous power in the hands of evil, I immediately returned to the cell where I was serving my sentence alongside two other inmates, the bad climate that existed between us disappeared, everything was a huge calm, I no longer saw any shadow of the dark ones circulating there.

I lay down on the narrow bunk bed and kept thinking about everything that happened, how I escaped with my life, I started to worry about the Queen, the fact that she came to meet me to avoid my death that was already certain was something intriguing, why would I have done that?

Demo was very clear in saying that he would not send me any help or the slightest deliverance, how is it that she suddenly appears out of nowhere, ordering the end of torture? Would he have reversed his decision to crush my body and take my captive soul to the darkest places in his kingdom to pay for my affront there?

No, that would be practically impossible, I humiliated him before his subordinates, I needed to regain prestige before him so that they would respect him again. I honestly kept asking myself for some time the reasons that led that demon with the appearance of a prostitute to help me.

Would she have fallen in love with me because we were so complete in bed? Why, what nonsense, and are the inhabitants of darkness equipped with the capacity to love? That nothing, pure speculation completely idiotic, to think about it was the biggest bullshit that had ever appeared in my mind, maybe it was because I was beaten too much in the head and was varying in ideas. Nowadays not even human beings can truly love one another.

Much less a devil like that, made of pure evil, as I was lying down, thinking too much, I ended up dozing, then again I left the body and was taken to the depths of the earth, in the darkness where there is the kingdom of the evil one. A tremendous force tore my soul away, leading it in that direction as if to answer an urgent call.

Or to see something that happened there, to my surprise, I found myself exactly in the spacious corridor that led to the throne of the ugly animal through which many children of darkness passed, heading towards the royal room, however, they seemed not to notice my presence. When I realized this, I went on, through all of them, until I got to the Evil One. It was a trial, someone from the kingdom had committed a serious fault against his king and should be punished, so the sentence was given:

— For disobeying the determinations of his king, preventing the execution of the one who for his decision should be tortured to death, his wife, the Queen of Evil, committed treason and now will pay for his rebellion!

According to the norms described in the supreme law of this kingdom, the demon known in the world of the living as “Pomba Gira” or “Jezabel”.

The greatest of all prostitutes, and among the demons as "Queen of Evil", for his boldness in disobeying the determinations. Imposed by the highest authority of this kingdom must be tortured for a century until our king's wrath is appeased! Let that sentence be served immediately! The dark spirit dressed in the clothes of a judge gave her ultimatum.

Immediately the soldiers of the kingdom took her to the beginning of the torture she would suffer for ten decades. That cut me inside, because everything would have been because of me, but I could do nothing to avoid such suffering, because I didn't have the necessary power to deliver it. What if I surrender in your place?

It would be enough to agree that my physical body would be killed and my soul would be theirs. I would go to torture in the lowest parts of hell and she would be forgiven or banished from the kingdom. Yes, that seemed to be the best way out at that moment, so I went to the Evil One's throne and offered him my offer.

But he and no one there seemed to see or hear me, I screamed so loudly that the echoes of my words would awaken the entire kingdom, but to no avail, an invisible barrier prevented the sound of my voice from crossing, reaching his ears.

Tired of trying in vain, I shut up, so I understood why, it was she who transported me in hell to the spirit at the very moment when I was being judged, made a point of showing the price she would be willing to pay for me, for my life. I accompanied my hot friend to her final destination, I could see the beginning of her suffering in the penalty that would last a hundred years according to the count of the spiritual world.

Which would certainly be much less if calculated in the world of the living. I didn't have enough time to watch all his martyrdoms, but I still saw a lot. That demon could feel the same pain as a human being, I say that with all certainty because I had already gone through all that once, as I said before, it is the soul or spirit that feels each martyrdom on the skin.

If someone goes to a wake and pinches a dead person he will feel nothing, because his soul has already left him, his body is lifeless, empty. This is, without a shadow of a doubt, the greatest proof that we are not just made of matter, but the existence of the human soul is the purest truth. In the distance he heard his screams filled with terror.

As she went through several stages of torture, she was burned alive, drowned in the rotten mud of the pits of hell, hung by her feet, placed upside down ...They pulled her nails from her feet and hands, she was beaten, kicked and kicked all over her body, tore her clothes, showed her shame, raped her dozens of times.

Abused her beautiful body to the limit of her strength. .All of this happened momentarily, changing from one scenario to another, like a dream, nothing was real. But for the spirit in question it seems to be all true because the pain felt is terrible, it gives the impression that it is happening in the physical body.

For this reason both Satan with his legions of demons and all the souls imprisoned in his kingdom will spend all eternity in a lake of fire created by God for that purpose, they will burn forever. I was still watching the Queen's suffering at the hands of her oppressors, when I heard her voice in my ears, telling me not to worry.

Because all that would be fleeting, it would soon be over. He told me that he would send me back to the world of the living, that he would have taken me there only to show how much he cared for me. Although my eyes saw her in complete despair at the hands of the cruel executioners, her voice sounded calm and serene to me.

Which surprised me, but she said that soon we would be together again, so she would explain to me how everything works in her world. . Yes, the Queen really had a great admiration and affinity for me. It was no wonder, since our moments of desire were complete and intense, that spirit dominated women.

Gave herself up in my arms in such a way that we almost burned the bed and the blankets. I never met another person with such potential in my life. I understood that only those who let themselves be possessed by evil are hot. With her I learned that sexual tara is a brilliant and necessary feature for a couple to complete and be happy.

However, it is a characteristic of the “Pombas Giras” of this world, of those who allow themselves to be dominated by evil, by carnal passions, by direct influence of the Queen of prostitutes. Without her in their lives they will be nothing more than horny women, after returning from the depths of the earth I found myself again inside that damn cell next to the two cronies who were overcome by evil and tried to kill me.

They were sitting on their beds, talking about something I couldn't understand, but their looks indicated that they planned to give pursuing the desire to take my life. Taking this particular into account, I began to reflect on how long I would remain alive there.

Since my defender would be paying for his blame in hell without being able to come to my aid, but God or destiny had already prepared everything about me. And in at the right time they would manifest themselves with the necessary deliverance to avoid the worst. I sat on the thin foam mattress that detainees are usually given to sleep in that kind of place.

Sty without taking their attention away from me in order to protect myself from a supposed attack, however. Aware that nothing I did would prevent me from taking another one. spanking, since they were big and without the power given by the demons it would not exist. It was noon, lunchtime.

All the prisoners were supposed to go to the cafeteria where I would undoubtedly be at risk of life again, so I let them go first, only after seeing them all sitting at their proper tables. I dared to take the food tray, but my strategy came to nothing, as I passed in the direction of one of the seats, one of the detainees put his leg in front of me to trip.

Falling on his face on the floor. The food tray shattered on the floor with me and everything was lost, I got up without saying anything while they laughed at my fall. I went back to the cell hungry, because the rule there was very clear, if the detainee lost his food, he would only eat the next day, he would be hungry, so I stayed there without any other way. Notwithstanding what happened earlier that afternoon.

They planned to kill me before nightfall, so when they returned to the cell they found me lying down. And suddenly launched themselves at me, one of them, the stronger of the two tried to choke me by grabbing my neck too hard while the other punched my stomach.

He certainly wouldn't resist another beating if no help came. Suddenly there was an inexplicable blackout, it was like night and the light had been turned off. They stopped beating me in amazement when a strong light appeared in the darkness that formed, then a colored circle appeared from where a brilliant being came out.

He was a tall man, dressed in white clothes made of the purest fabric, with a cross-shaped chest in the shape of an X, made of gold, at the waist was a wide shiny belt, in his right hand a very sharp sword, his hair was white as snow and his eyes like flames of fire, by knowing the Holy Scriptures at once I identified that mysterious being.

And concluded that finally my cry to the Creator had been answered, before him the two criminals fell into a faint, as for me, who was in the position of a victim, I felt nothing abnormal in his presence, however, out of respect and reverence I knelt at his feet, worshiping him. He, touching my chin with his sword, lifted me up, causing me to stand up to hear him:

"Stand up in my presence, a man of great faith, because your prayers have reached my ears and will now be answered, your deliverance will be accomplished according to what you asked for, because you have great value for me! I have followed your struggle since I was just a child, you have lived in this world for several existences.

In all of them you have committed many crimes and for that reason you have never returned home. In the beginning you were one of my heavenly princes, one of the most valiant in my Kingdom, however, you decided to come and live on earth, occupying the human form in order to be able to help your fellow men.

It turns out that when he was inside a mortal body he lost the memory of who he had been before, allowing himself to be dominated by carnal desires. Your ambition led you to commit many mistakes, crimes, barbarities that we are ashamed of today, but we do not prevent you from having your free will.

The possibility of choosing your own path in the world that you chose to inhabit. For various incarnations you have only practiced evil and for it you have had pleasure, for that reason I cast you into the most complete darkness. There you became the son of the evil one and opposed to your God, he lost the fellowship he once had with me.

He became a lover of darkness, he became trapped in the darkness of sin, you were cursed for various incarnations. However, at the worst moment of this current existence you cried out for myself without completely remembering your past or who you really are. So I am here to help you, to free you from the clutches of the Evil One, to give you the peace you need so much.

As I like to give you another chance to return home. From now on, Satan will not touch you, at the gates of hell he will not overcome you, rise before me and take back all the power you have lost, may all the glory from before fall on you!

As if by magic, incomparable glory descended on me and my appearance as a simple sinner fell apart, I was dressed like a warrior. A sharp and shiny sword appeared in my right hand, over my head something similar to a helmet, in my left hand a shield, I felt my hair growing even below my shoulders.

There was a loud crash and in the blink of an eye I was no longer in that filthy cell, we were transported to a brightly lit place, surrounded by light, brightness, different colors. A crowd made up of thousands of other beings just like you transformed me into. they waited, greatly glorifying the name of our God. They all sang in one voice:

"Lift up your heads, O gates, arise, O eternal gates, and the King of Glory will come in! Who is this King of Glory? It is the Lord our God who created the heavens and the earth with all that is in them! "

Seeing them, I immediately understood who that powerful being was who rescued me from that hell and what I had become. I had been transformed into a heavenly angel likewise to all those who praised his return to Heaven. He was Jesus Christ, the son of the Eternal, I had the honor of being rescued by God Himself, taken back to my old home to live with my brothers, brave fighters against the evil that dominates the earth, servants of the Creator.

When we entered through the immense doors of the grand palace accompanied by the Royal Guard, we followed the wide corridor, stepping on a red carpet with details in pure gold, everything there was covered with the most valuable precious stones. The atmosphere was soft, calm, well lit, a golden peace was felt, so beautiful and charming.

The gracious being who welcomed me was dressed in a shining garment, covered with pearls, rubies, sapphire and other glittering stones, then led by his servants to a throne made of gold, there he sat to rule his Kingdom. He called me to his presence to once again hear his words that would make me surprising revelations.

Fifth Chapter - Archangels and Demons

After the long conversation with the celestial being, I became aware that he was the Son of the Most High and I was one of the brave princes of that wonderful Kingdom of Glowing glory. There was a time when he, like me, decided to go down to earth and lived there for a little more than three decades, taking human form.

He tried to teach men about faith in a holy, pure, true God, able to free them from the bonds of sin, but their worst enemy, Satan, the father of lies, deceit and responsible for the moral degradation of humanity used all his devices to condemn him to death, taking him to the cross.

However, what that disgusting pig snout did not know was that it would only be contributing to the conclusion of the divine plan in which a perfect and sinless man would die for the benefit of humanity. Pouring his pure blood on a rude cross that at that time was considered the most inhuman and shameful death penalty applied to someone.

His name in physical form was Jesus Christ, the Savior, Messiah ... Because of his sacrifice even today thousands of people still follow and teach his doctrine, the Gospel of Grace, the Good News of Salvation to men and through faith many souls have already been freed there. All of them have their names written in the Lamb's Book of Life and Satan can no longer touch them, as he has lost the power he wielded over their lives.

Also, my Lord, it reminded me of who I was, my importance and worth in your Kingdom, I remembered all the things that for three generations lived on earth remained hidden from my mind. The queen, along with the other four demons, made me believe that he was the son of the Devil, but it was all a tremendous mistake forged by the father of lies.

Actually because I had committed many sins during the three incarnations on earth. I was handed over to the Evil One who, taking advantage of my spiritual amnesia, lied to me. Yes, I have sinned so many times that the Creator decided to leave me in this world to be swallowed up by physical and spiritual death.

Closed the gates of heaven and would no longer allow me to return unless I somehow regret my bad deeds, which I did the moment I prayed in an agonizing way, believing in the existence of a higher power. My heavenly name is Michael Archangel, I am the leader of the Archangels the greatest legion of warrior angels in the Kingdom of my God.

It was me with my brothers who fought a strong battle against the ancient serpent, the Devil, expelling him from the celestial mansions, when he in the company of thousands of other Cherubim tried to invade and take the Throne of the Most High.

And there was a battle in heaven; Michael and his angels battled the dragon, and battled the dragon and his angels. But they did not prevail, nor was their place found in the heavens. And the great dragon, the ancient serpent, called the Devil, and Satan, who deceives the whole world. Was precipitated; he was precipitated on the earth, and his angels were cast with him, yes, the old name of Satan, before his fall, was Lucifer.

He was an angel of great glory and power, responsible for the praise and worship of God, singing teacher, an Anointed Cherub to give his Creator due worship. However, one day he let himself be taken by exaltation and sinned by wanting to take the place of the Most High and was condemned to hell.

Lucifer's sentence was given by the Almighty in the presence of the entire Heavenly Kingdom, as follows:

"You were in Eden, the garden of God; your covering was of all precious stones: sardonia, topaz, diamond, turquoise, onyx, jasper, sapphire, carbuncle, emerald and gold; your drums and your fife were made in you; on the day you were created they were prepared.

You were the cherubim, anointed to cover, and I established you; on the holy mountain of God you were walking among the flushed stones.

You were perfect in your ways, from the day you were created, until iniquity was found in you.

In the multiplication of your trade they filled your interior with violence, and you sinned; therefore, I threw you, profaned, from the mountain of God, and made you perish, O covering cherub, from among the flushed stones.

Your heart was lifted up because of your beauty, you corrupted your wisdom because of your radiance; I threw you down to the earth, before the kings I set you, so that they may look at you. By the multitude of your iniquities, by the injustice of your trade, you have profaned your sanctuaries.

I therefore caused a fire to come out of you, which consumed you and made you ashes on the earth, in the eyes of all who see you. All who know you among the peoples are astonished at you; in great amazement you have become, and will never survive. "

In this way, we understand that Satan is revolted for having lost his glory with all the benefits he enjoyed in the presence of the Most High, for being one of the first inhabitants of the Garden of Eden and then seeing him being inhabited by the first couple of human beings, when he was banned from living there, he did everything to get them expelled from there.

Demo is the father of lies, deception and responsible for human death, because the divine plan was for man to be eternal, there would be no end to his existence on earth. The rebelliousness of the first human beings in the garden allowed the entry of evil, through sin, into this world, ending the permanent life covenant with man.

Soon after remembering who I was, as well as my importance as a defender of the Kingdom of my God, I was replaced in my former role as leader of the heavenly warriors. The Lord of Hosts summoned me to a meeting, where he asked what I would like to do on my first mission as an Archangel after three hundred years away from the Kingdom.

Without hesitating, I proposed to my Lord to return to the land to wage an intense battle against Satan to devastate his kingdom, annihilate his power over human beings, free the captive souls and with that release the Queen, a demon who despite inciting me to practice sexual sin helped me a lot.

He gave me such permission, but on condition that he would only release her if she was in full agreement to abandon the practice of evil through true repentance, sincerely humbling herself before the Creator of life and the Father of all spirits. I agreed to propose that proposal to her, and then left in the company of ten legions of angels.

At the same time that the celestial army descended towards the earth, Satan was informed of the attack by his allies who inhabit the four corners of the planet and gathered his best warriors, sending them into space in order to prevent the invaders from reaching their destination. Kingdom.

A battle like never before in the history of the spirit world took place between heaven and earth without human beings being aware of it, there was thunder, earthquakes, storms, the waters of the seas became violent and a third of life on the plantation was devastated, several catastrophes culminated in disorder, death and destruction.

However, the defending forces of the kingdom of darkness were no match to prevent the advance of the Archangels, who in addition to being in greater numbers were endowed with greater power for having the protection of the Most High who retains sovereign power over the entire Universe, being easily defeated in combat.

Realizing that his legions of demons had failed to prevent the advance of heavenly troops into his kingdom, the Devil, the ancient serpent, the worst enemy of God, rose from his throne, gathered hundreds of thousands of his most powerful combatants and left in person to face his opponents. The encounter of these with the angels of light still in the air was felt by humanity through radical changes in nature with more earthquakes.

Storms, hurricanes, landslides, catastrophes ... In their natural disbelief, scientists believed that all those events were fruits climatic conditions, greenhouse effect, changes in the atmosphere ... They didn't even know what actually happened, scientific skepticism and the incredulity of most of humanity lead to disbelief in what happens on the spiritual plane.

Making them blind to the true reality of what happens in outer space. The battle between angels and demons took weeks, months, in a duel where the fighting power between both sides was put to the test, I placed myself at the head of the heavenly armies.

Leading the Archangels in the battle against the enemies of God, while the ancient Cherubim, Lucifer, commanded his legions of fallen angels against our insistence on invading his dark kingdom. Hundreds of them came to confront me directly at the behest of the wicked, he feared that with all the power that was given to me he would be able to defeat them.

Easily alone, even more counting on my brothers Archangels who were no less worthy warriors than me. I was hailed as the most powerful Angel in the heavens and for that reason I was given the honor of leading them, but they were all excellent, worthy of respect for their bravery, in the history of God's people, Israel.

I have always been the one sent to fight evil and defeat it, I am the guardian of that nation until today and for that reason the gates of hell never prevailed against it. I was before them when they left Egypt after four hundred years of slavery under the wrath of Pharaoh, who was instructed by the evil one to subdue it. It was I, at the behest of the Lord, who opened the Red Sea for Moses and more than three million Jews passed through.

Stepping on dry ground, without any danger. I walked before them through the desert, kept their lives, pointed out the path for them to follow, fed them with Manna and gave them several books during the arduous walk. Whenever other nations bigger and more powerful than Israel tried to destroy it.

I was sent by the Creator in order to free it from the hands of enemies. I was the one who passed through the Assyrian camp, in the times of the prophet Isaiah, destroying King Sennacherib's army of one hundred thousand men, passing with my sword drawn over his camp. I was on that mountain where Moses, servant of the Most High God.

Died, defending his body so that he was not taken to hell by the Temptor, I confronted Lucifer in the battle on the day he dared to challenge my God and threw him up and down. I am a warrior prince, leader of the Archangels, anointed by the Almighty to always fight and win, Satan knows this.

And has tried to keep me trapped in this world as a simple human being in order to prevent me from somehow destroying his kingdom of sin, because despite the coming of Christ he still remained the god of the earth, his dominion over the earth. humanity continued as it was before, but now it would come to an end.

My mistake in the past was wanting to imitate my Lord, because when I saw him leave his kingdom of glory in the heavens, descend into this world, become a natural man to give his life on the cross for sinners, enabling their redemption with their Father me I felt like doing something similar to help the man fallen into sin.

However, I was prevented from doing this with divine permission, my plan had not been approved by Heavenly Father and it saddened me greatly. But I decided to go ahead with my ideas, meeting my Lord's will, acting on my own. So, I received as a punishment the forgetfulness of my origins as soon as I incarnated and was born of a woman on earth.

I grew up without knowing who I really was or why I was here. My powers as an Archangel were taken away, my memory erased, I became a normal child like all the others, I was born into a poor family, without education, incredulous ... A sorcerer father, envious brothers, a mother who loved me.

But without the strength to defend me in the face of the abyss that opened before me, hell followed me from my earliest childhood and I was influenced by him in this third existence after having already lived other incarnations where I committed innumerable insanities, after rebelling against the kingdom of darkness.

I was persecuted in human form and I just did not die because I counted on the help of the Evil Queen, wife of Satan, who decided to join me, betraying his countrymen. Trapped inside that maximum security detention house, surrounded by all kinds of criminals, I escaped with my life out of mercy.

When hell arose and determined that once again I would be pulled out of my physical body, the Eternal God remembered the prayer he had made in the midst of darkness and sent his only Son in person to rescue me from the imminent end, taking me back to my old place, returning my memory, restoring the glory I threw away.

God is merciful and always willing to grant us forgiveness for our transgressions, despite the unbelief of some on earth, he never refuses to extend his hands to free, heal, save ... Even though I was an Angel of high position in heaven I committed the serious sin of the rebellion, because I disobeyed his orders, but I had a second chance.

In the case of Lucifer, his act was so serious that his sentence led him straight to eternal condemnation, he no longer has the right to repent, our God has hardened his heart to the point that he cannot repent of his iniquities. When a creature reaches this stage in life, what remains is eternal fire.

The fight between angels and demons in outer space lasted for a long time, since neither side nor the other can die, victory in a battle like this occurs when one of the opponents gives up the fight and flees before the enemy. Like the other Archangels, under my leadership they were more powerful, without ever giving up, they won.

The Devil, the ancient serpent of Eden, together with his demons decided to retreat, allowing us to pass through the barrier created by them at the entrance of the atmosphere. We continued in pursuit of those who went down to the depths of the land where the kingdom of darkness was, our goal was to devastate everything there.

As we imagined great legions of all kinds of demons and unclean spirits that lived in the dark, they armed themselves and came to face us as soon as we got there. However, even Satan calling everyone as much as he could to help him, promising redemption for souls captive for their many sins is of no avail.

The Evil One's despair was so great when he saw us invade hell with our intense light that he joined a battalion of condemned people to fight against heavenly beings endowed with high glory, forgetting that nothing and no one in this mortal world can overcome them. Only our immense aura dissipated them. If the other fallen angels who followed Satan from the beginning, endowed with a certain power, were no match to defeat us how much simpler lost souls would do that.

While my subordinates gave a tremendous beating on the subjects of the Demo, he and I had a private fight inside his amazing castle, in the place where he reigned. We use all kinds of methods to win in that dispute, from corporal fight to the use of different types of weapons capable of waning beings with supernatural powers. However, nothing leads us to fall to the ground or the performance in front of the opponent, we were two tireless warriors in the ideal of taking the best.

— Do not think that this time it will be easy to defeat me!

— I have beaten you countless times over the course of several centuries, what could make things different now?

— With the passing of so many Ages I ended up becoming stronger, but you on the other hand, stayed three generations in this world without having the slightest idea of who you were, believing in the lies that my subjects and I told you. There were three reincarnations where we made you commit so many atrocities that I don't even understand how your God still granted you forgiveness, I should have let you rot in that prison and give me your spirit to be punished in the darkness, what is certain is that he lost much of your power as an Archangel.

And today he is no longer able to defeat me in a fair fight!

— That's what we'll see!

After this brief conversation, we returned to the confrontation that shook that damn place. My opponent was right about what he said. I lost a lot of my power because I stayed on earth so long, living with human beings, descending and rising from hell between physical death and each new reincarnation. But when he was reestablished in the Kingdom of my God he gave me all the necessary energy to successfully accomplish that mission.

If in space the battle between good and evil took a long time, resulting in several catastrophes in nature in the deepest part of the earth, it could not be different, volcanoes deactivated for hundreds of years have again expelled their lava and melted all the surrounding vegetation, as well as causing real damage with the destruction of several cities. With each attack on the various sectors of the kingdom of Satan, the earth shook in various parts of the world, people were frightened, looking for answers in the wrong places for not taking into account the existence of an underground world where darkness reigns, place where all those who mock the Living God and his Son Jesus Christ will go.

My armies waged a real war against the evil forces within the empire itself, Satan's wrath was so great that he used his power to torment human beings because he understood that only in this way would God order our departure from his kingdom because he was too concerned with the people, works of their hands. However, this was not how things happened, the more he sent his subjects to send plagues.

Diseases, viruses and all kinds of diseases on humanity, the Most High crossed his arms, doing nothing to defend them, ordering us to continue with our fight. against the damned rebellious angel, along with his legion of demons. Various forms of disease have arisen on earth that have caused the death of millions of people, a lethal virus has appeared in the four corners of the planet.

Consuming a third of human beings through air contamination, causing the multiple failure of their vital organs for survival, nor science or medicine was able to stop the killing. In this same period when we were fighting the greatest spiritual battle that can be remembered, humanity suffered the worst phase of its existence.

With terrible catastrophes that are still remembered for generations, it was they, hundreds of them that culminated with a large part of the world population. Among others, we can mention the HIV and the Corona Virus that killed millions of people in a few months, besides the First and Second World War.

In these last two cases, Satan used powerful men on the planet to start a battle between human beings themselves, in order to kill themselves, advancing their service of mass destruction. Among the most perverse we can quote Adolfo Hitler as the incarnation of one of the sounds of Satan.

The one Joseph who swore he was my brother, the son of my human parents in the last incarnation and who appeared to me all the time dressed in that green military uniform and tattered, but in fact it was put there to control me towards evil. He incarnated being born in Germany where he became the creator of the Neo Nazi Party.

And then was directly responsible for the beginning of the Second World War, with the death of millions of innocent people, including Jews whom Satan always hated for being the chosen Nation of our God, thus the Satanic plans were confirmed. The battle between the angels of God against demons took place on the spiritual plane while all these terrible things happened up there on the surface, it took us a long time to overcome the damned, but finally we managed to defeat them with the coming of the Son of the Most High in person to help us, I feared that only with my sword I would not defeat him.

— I am happy to see you here, my Lord!

— I let you and your combatants face this fight against these demons alone to improve you in the fight, after all, you spent a long time without fighting. However, undoubtedly not even with all the war training you have, your skills and power as an Archangel of greater magnitude will be able to overcome this enemy, because only me has such merit. Now move away, Miguel, I am destined to destroy this damn demon!

— Yes sir!

I obeyed, leaving immediately, going to help my brothers in another part of the immense kingdom of Satan, because they needed my help to exterminate once and for all our enemies that still resisted strongly.

— So the one we killed on the Cross still lives?

— That's right, as you see I didn't die, just my human body you martyred and crucified there! However, after the third day I was resurrected, returning to my Father's house.

Resuming my former status as King of kings and Lord of Lords throughout the universe!

— Well now the time has come for our fine combat, this time you will die!

The struggle between light and darkness began. With each blow to the wicked one, the Lord passed his sharp sword through Satan's scaly body, which tried in vain to avoid the voracious attack of my God. Even in another part of that realm helping the other Archangels, I could see the battle waged between those two immortals.

The sound caused by the impact of their weapons sounded loud and it was possible to hear it from a great distance, lightning and thunder shook the place, the two mortal enemies seemed like two gladiators determined to win the challenge at any price.

In the same way we, the Archangels, were tireless in the confrontation, so we overcame God's enemies. Defeated, they surrendered, then were chained and taken into the chains where they held souls condemned for their sins, they remain there today. The last to be overcome was the king of darkness who finally fell at the feet of our God, admitting his failure before the Almighty.

— Archangels, all standing before the Son of the Most High!

— Yes sir!

— I want to acknowledge here the great importance that each of you demonstrated to have before your Lord, who entrusted to you this valiant mission of destroying the action of the Evil One and his demons.

Know that our victory today will make a huge difference in the life of mankind, since the whole earth had been devastated by the worst catastrophes, epidemics, incurable diseases. Many innocent people lost their lives while fighting this battle against evil, but it all came to an end thanks to the interference of all of us in this world. Satan, the enemy of the Father and his people is vanquished, imprisoned, captive within the chains of his own kingdom of death, here he will spend a thousand years in captivity.

Then it will be launched into the great Lake of Fire that my Father and I have prepared for him, his demons and for all who decide to follow him in his rebellion. As for you, brave warriors, as well as all who have believed my words, abandoning evil, following good, will be worthy to dwell forever in the heavenly mansions.

Eternity will be eternity with me and my Father, we will be your God, they will be heirs to the glory to come, they will never be abandoned, together with the Cherubim, side by side with my Bride, the Church that will be taken from the earth on that Last Day , will glorify the Almighty, the Creator of all things visible or invisible.

After this conversation with the Son of the Most High satan was chained and trapped in the filthy ditches of his own world of darkness, the Lord announced the opportunity to forgive the thousands of lost souls who have been held there since the time of the Flood, who have not had the chance to meet or hear him during his stay on earth as a man. Those who acknowledged their mistakes, admitting that they themselves were guilty of being there.

He forgave them and on returning to heaven he took them with him, como afirmam as Escrituras que testificam sobre seus feitos neste mundo, quando diz: “Levou consigo o cativeiro!”. Nós, eu e os demais Arcanjos, permanecemos mais uns dias naquele buraco.

Nosso objetivo era ter certeza de que nenhum demônio ficaria livre das cadeias eternas, revisando cada cela, confirmando suas amarras. Não esqueci da Rainha e sai à sua procura por todo o território infernal, encontrando-a no final do lugar, amarrada dentro de um fosso profundo, cheio de imundícies.

Tive compaixão daquele demônio e lhe propus a condição imposta pelo meu Deus a fim de que pudesse garantir sua salvação, ela teria que se arrepender de todos os atos de imoralidade praticado durante suas várias encarnações, tentar concertá-los praticando boas ações na terra entre os viventes através de uma sincera humilhação.

Não difícil convencê-la a aceitar a proposta divina e em pouco tempo já estávamos no Paraíso diante do Todo Poderoso para fosse feito seu julgamento pelo Grande Juiz. Depois de julgada, condenada, porém perdoada, ela recebeu a oportunidade de novamente reencarnar na terra como ser humano, outra vez uma mulher, porém decente e pura.

Final Chapter - Redemption

Heavenly Father's forgiveness given to the Queen of evil allowed her to be purified of all the influence of the Evil One who was buried together with his demons in the depths of the earth, chained within the pits created for souls condemned for loving sin more than holiness God's.

Both Satan and his fallen angels, as well as the lost souls, would remain in the chains of hell for hundreds of years, but she, the former wife of the Evil One, who for several centuries influenced many people, both men and women to prostitute herself, was transformed into a new creature, by permission of the Creator.

She stopped wearing extravagant clothes, stripped of the appearance of a prostitute and dressed in fine linen like all the other saints who lived in Paradise, the other souls who decided to convert to the Son of the Most High, when he preached them their Gospel right after defeating the Demo in their kingdom of darkness.

All of them were taken by him to the heavens and there they started to worship him day and night together with the Cherubim, the old "Pomba Gira", mother of prostitutes, now he would be a being of light who would reincarnate on earth to atone for good their sins committed in previous existences, through penance in this world of mortals. In this way, the Eternal Father sent her back to earth and she would be born again.

That beautiful child would have a painful childhood, her parents would be poor, she would learn to live with material poverty. Hunger, misery, injustice ... But in the end she would grow up with a strong personality, love for his fellow men would burn in his chest, that woman would become an example of love.

Mercy and compassion for her neighbor, dedicate her whole new existence to reach out to the most needy, give them all of herself. Her name could be remembered by future generations as a saint who never measured efforts to enable the happiness of the weakest, Holy Mother Teresa would bring to the world the light he needed to escape from the darkness.

Left by the influence of Satan and his demons while dominating this planet, however nothing would be easily conquered, enormous difficulties she would encounter during her almost one century of permanence in this existential plan, hus, after being revealed to her what her new mission on this planet would be.

She decidedly agreed and so the whole plan outlined by the Creator came to fruition, the child was born on August 26, 1910 in Albania, from an early age dedicated to religious life on behalf of the poor and has since done great things for them. Her dedication in favor of the poorest classes gave her international renown, taking her prestige to all the Continents.

Covering the four corners of the earth, receiving the Nobel Peace Prize, being beatified as a truly holy woman by Catholicism, but her greatest feat was the demonstration of love for others. He passed away before the age of ninety after fulfilling all his goal in the mission received from the Eternal Father, returning to the Kingdom of God as a pure,

Enlightened and deserving of our acceptance, during the time she was doing her penance on earth, I was at her side in spirit, freeing her from countless dangers in her journey, all the intimate involvement that once existed in having both of us was erased from our history and as it remained in chastity throughout the last existence, without ever having been touched by a man.

It was also expiated from this guilt, purifying itself from such acts, so the Father of Lights enlightened her to the point that she became a stronghold in the heavens. As for me, I remained as leader of the Archangels for two centuries until I was entrusted with a new opportunity to return to the world of mortals.

I would be born into a family of many possessions, but that would never give any importance to social standards, causing great sadness to my parents. Once again, forgetting my heavenly origins, I would have the chance to correct pending issues left in the past where I ended up harming my fellow men.

As long as I lived among mortals Gabriel, one of my brothers better prepared than the rest in battle, would take my place in leading the Archangels until I returned. Remembering that there is a big difference in time between the spiritual and the material world, therefore, a century in this world is not more than a few years there.

Thus I was born in the United Kingdom, my baptismal name was chosen by Bishop Monsignor Francisco, an important papal representative. I was called BEDA, which means PRAYER. There I grew up and since I was a teenager I disagreed with Catholic doctrine and its idolatry.

Because I dedicated myself to the study of the Holy Bible, becoming profoundly aware of divine truths. I remembered nothing of my life in heaven with God, but I felt an enormous love for everything I learned in Scripture regarding the Creator of life. Because of my constant rebellions against my parents' idolatrous faith and the infamous doctrine of the church. I was prevented from continuing to be accepted as a devotee of Mary, cursed by the bishops, expelled from the communion of the so-called "Christians". At twenty years of age, after reaching the limit of bad family life, I decided to leave the house.

— You can't insist on this pointless stubbornness, my son!

— I am sorry my mother, but I will not give in to my father's whims, I have a different faith than you have and I will not submit to having to deny it in order to live with the family

— We gave you the best education, a wealthy life, nothing was ever lacking, I don't understand the reason for so much rebellion!

— Do not try to understand my reasons, Mom, I just feel that I need to find my space in this world, I feel that here with you it is not my place, as much as the material wealth that you gave me does not matter to me, because while we live in abundance many families are starving the world out

— My son we are not responsible for the world's misery

— Your way of looking at life is selfish, my mother, Christ taught us to love our fellowmen!

—Yes, and because of that, he ended up on a cross!

— Your thoughts are the same as that of Dad.

And all the other image-worshipers in this damn city, so I will be going far away from all of you!

— Don't forget that it was these image worshipers, as you just mentioned, who paid for their studies at the best schools and colleges in this country!

— I am grateful, but in my opinion you as my parents did not do more than your duty, now excuse me I need to pack my bags, because I want to leave today

— Where are you going, how will you support yourself from now on, if after leaving that door your father will no longer pay your expenses?

— Rest assured, I will be able to survive with the savings that I still have

— And after you finish doing what? Will you work like a poor wretch to make a living?

— I do not know, maybe...

— Good God, my son, stop this madness for good!

I went from the room where we were talking to my room with the intention of packing my bags, at that very moment my father came home and still heard Mom's last words

— What conversation is this woman?

— Our son has gone crazy, my husband, he's leaving!

— Is that true, BEDA? Do you really want to leave your family in exchange for a risky and meaningless adventure?

Yes, that's right. The only thing that is not correct is that you call my choice of life an adventure and something meaningless. I am not venturing out, my father, I just chose a path to follow other than the one you have outlined for me, because each one of us is free to decide his future

— How dare you call such a stupid and hasty choice of the future? What do you think you will find at the end of this unknown road that you intend to follow if it is not misery and destruction?

— It may be my father, but we will never know if I stand here without taking the first steps towards the unknown

— Where did this adventurous spirit come from? Surely me and your mother did not go!

— I believe it was God who gave it to me. Besides, it's not about adventure, Dad, it's about freedom. Ever since I was a child I have been bound by the dogmas of this evil idolatrous religion and now I must live my true faith

— But what faith are you talking about, boy? Is there another saint greater than our mother, Maria?

— Show me in the Holy Scriptures that this Mary of Nazareth occupies some position of power and glory in heaven? That she is a goddess capable of saving, healing, freeing or throwing the human soul into hell? But I can do that, I show you where it is written that Jesus Christ can do all these things!

— Very well, I understand everything, you must be getting involved with these rebels who fight our holy church and misrepresent the truth!

— Who, the reformers?

— Who else would they be? Are they not responsible for disorder in the church when they accuse our priests and bishops of exploiting our people?

— They are not responsible for the infamy preached by the idolaters in this country, they are responsible for the revelation of the truth!

— But what truth are you talking about, boy? Since when is opposing Rome wise and true? To buy a fight with the Pope is to sign his death certificate, the balance of this type of rebellion is death!

— Okay, no doubt that's why you all humble yourself at your feet! They are cowards and are afraid to die by the sword of these corrupt Romans!

— Look here, you respect us, because you are still inside this house!

— True, my father, for this reason I will leave your property right now

— My son think about your decision!

— Stay calm, mom, I've thought enough

— Know that as soon as you leave this house you will not be able to return, you will no longer be accepted as my son!

— Don't worry my father, I won't be back

Without understanding the real reasons for being a young man different from the others of my time who only valued material riches, lust and a life full of pleasures.

That morning I turned my back on everything apparently valuable and started off towards the unknown, from there on. a new cycle would begin in my existence. He had been sent to earth with an important mission, that of fighting for the Gospel. of Christian truths, he would suffer the martyrdom necessary to bring humanity to the knowledge of his Redeemer.

However, nothing would be that easy, because despite Satan and his demons being trapped in the depths of hell, evil still existed on earth. Sometimes we look at the evil that dominates mankind and cast total blame on the Devil, forgetting that there is a strong and growing root of evil that expands within man himself.

Leading him to reject God, despise the good, choose to practice of iniquity instead of wanting to unite with your Creator. That root of evil that still exercises its power of dominion over humanity is the sin that entered this world there in Eden, when the Devil used the serpent to deceive the woman, convincing him to eat the forbidden fruit and then convincing the man to disobey the Creator's ordinances.

No matter whether Satan is present or not in this world of mortals, sin will continue within your hearts, acting in the same intensity as before. This is what I discovered at high costs during the last incarnation on earth. To my surprise, I could see the spread of corruption in mankind, immorality, the growth of violence ...

I saw the death of innocents, the injustices, the misery, the hunger that punished so many civilizations, the expansion of the traffic, the uncontrollable use of drugs, the sexual immorality in its different phases, the apostasy of the faith.

On the part of those who once claimed to be believers in God, religious fanaticism, the death of millions of people who decided to remain faithful, then I realized that sin and Satan are two separate, distinct beings. One is the creator of evil while the other is the executor of evil, one determines and the other puts into practice.

It was for this reason that I returned, God knew that there was still a trace of darkness on the earth to be destroyed, but only now do I realize it. Since the day I left home I never returned to see my parents again, as an only child he should be the heir to all his possessions, which were not few, but I preferred to leave them to the bishops of Rome or to anyone else.

I lived for almost a hundred years and fulfilled everything assigned to me even without understanding what my last mission as a man really was. This part of my story may tell you in another opportunity, now what I have left is to breathe relieved after all the martyrdom experienced as a defender of divine truths. Here, sitting on the peak of the highest mountain in this world where despite all the sacrifices made by all of us, heavenly beings.

Humanity continues to remain blind and without direction, what remains for me to ask myself is whether it was really worth so much suffering. From Christ until now what has changed in the behavior of mortal man? It hurts me a lot to see the Gospel corrupted, humanity lost and true faith confused with materialistic religions.

The And

Lightning Source UK Ltd.
Milton Keynes UK
UKIC010818101120
373113UK00012B/205

* 9 7 8 1 0 3 4 0 1 2 3 4 4 *